If I Told You

By
Avery Easton

Avery Easton

This is a work of fiction. Names, characters, places and events described herein are products of the author's imagination or are used fictitiously and are not to be construed as real. Any resemblance to actual events, locations, organizations, or persons, living or dead, is entirely coincidental.

ISBN 978-1-7373942-0-4

If I Told You
Copyright © 2021 by Carolyn Johnson

Cover art and design
Copyright © 2021 by Dorothy Ewald

All rights reserved. Except for use in review, the reproduction or utilization of this work in whole or in part in any form by any electronic, mechanical or other means now known or hereafter invented, is forbidden without the written permission of the publisher.

Warning: The unauthorized reproduction or distribution of this copyrighted work is illegal. Criminal copyright infringement, including infringement without monetary gain, is investigated by the FBI and is punishable by up to five (5) years in federal prison and a fine of $250,000.

Also available in eBook by Uncial Press, an imprint of GCT, Inc. Visit us at uncialpress.com

For all the Paiges: the artists, the villains, the drama queens, the lovers.

If you would like to enjoy the playlist that accompanies this novel, please search for *If I Told You* on your favorite music streaming site.

Spotify
Amazon
YouTube
Apple Music

ONE

My bag fell to the floor with a heavy thud and I leaned against the door for a moment, glad to be home. Turning to secure the locks, I felt a dull ache in my lower back and silently cursed my dance partner. The life of an aging dancer was one filled with dull aches, a reality I was starting to learn now that I was nearly thirty.

"Paige? You home?"

"Hey, Kat." I padded down the hall to her bedroom doorway where I leaned gratefully, tired but still buzzing from the matinee, then post-show dinner and drinks with my castmates.

Kat sat at her dressing table mirror, a podcast playing on her phone. She was old glam all the way, like a forties movie star. As I watched her carry out her beauty routine, we listened to the conversation coming from her phone, a stand-up comedian being interviewed by the host. The comfort of another night's end settled around us.

She raised a slender arm, graceful as a butterfly, and finished wrapping a satin scarf around her dreads. Kat wasa dancer like me, but so much better. Enchanting. She moved from the Joffrey Ballet in Chicago to the American Ballet here in New York.

I've always preferred jazz and contemporary. And I loved musical theater, which had landed me an ensemble role in a revival of *Cabaret* on Broadway. I loved the show, but I'd been performing in it for well over a year. It was getting close to the end of my contract, and I was trying to decide if I wanted to renew.

"So how did you know you were getting a little famous?" the podcast host asked.

"I was in the middle of Illinois," the guest replied, her voice husky and perfect for radio. "A guy with a camo hat told me he liked my set at a club I'd played the night before. Imagine me, this little queer, being approached by this big hunter at a gas station. I was so flattered I almost asked him out. But then I remembered... lesbian!"

I chuckled. Her comedic timing was great. "Who is that?"

"Her name is Alexandra Tate. I've never heard of her but she's charming."

"Mmm," I replied. We listened for a little while longer as Kat continued her skin care regimen. Alexandra Tate had laughter in her voice. I liked it.

Kat paused the podcast. "How was the show?"

I shook myself out from under the sound of Alexandra's husky voice. There was something so soothing about it that I'd gotten a little lost. "Same as always. Great audience today. Dev almost dropped me during the second act, which he hasn't done since rehearsals. I have never seen him more apologetic, but now my back is killing me. How was class?"

She threw me a pot of Aspercreme, a standard in our medicine cabinet. "It was good." Her voice hitched. From all the years we'd lived together, I knew her tics. She was hiding something.

"What happened?"

Kat turned and began delicately applying under-eye cream. She paused and met my eyes in the mirror. My expression was fierce, one eyebrow raised.

"Okay, okay. We went out for drinks after class and I ran into... Ethan."

I groaned and slid to the floor, my legs splayed out in front of me. I stretched over them, hoping for some relief to my back pain and also maybe to disappear and never hear the name Ethan again.

"That's a bit dramatic." Kat's voice dripped with sarcasm.

"Ethan makes me dramatic," I moaned into my knees.

"Don't I know it."

I whipped my head up and glared at her. Kat was the only person in my life that I let rag on me about Ethan.

Ugh.

Uggghhhh.

I groaned again and lay flat against my legs, gripping the arches of my feet. I could feel Kat staring at me, and I knew exactly what her expression said: *You brought this on yourself, get over it. And even though you're a little nuts, I still love you.*

I heard her move and pick up the cream where I'd dropped it. With the intimacy that all theater people have, she plopped down next to me, lifted my sweater, and rubbed the cream onto my lower back.

"Thank you." My face was still buried in my knees.

"Well. I used the last of yours yesterday."

I snorted. She really was the sister I never had. In the silence that followed, a siren went past the building. Joyous shrieking reached our second-floor window. Queens was alive tonight. Kat's strong hands slid along my back and moved my sweater back down. I sat up, sure my face was red.

"Are you going to make me ask what he said to you?"

A devious grin stole over her face. "Yep."

I swatted her arm and reached for one of her numerous pillows. I hugged it to my chest. Kat's room was warm, decorated with tapestries and throw pillows everywhere. The lamps were draped with scarves which created an intimate glow. I loved it in here. My own room seemed stark in comparison. I pouted at her.

"All right, I'll stop torturing you. We were at a bar. I saw his face. He caught my eye before I could avoid him, and you know he and I don't have any beef. So... what could I do? He actually came over to me. And we said *hi hello how are you great I'm fine*. The end. Really."

I felt humiliation bubble up inside my chest, as it did whenever I thought of the way I'd treated Ethan. Sometimes, when I looked back on how I acted at that time in my life, I couldn't believe I was the same person. What I'd done was inexcusable. It filled me with hot shame every time I thought about it.

I met Kat's eyes again.

She sighed. "He didn't ask about you."

"I know. Why the hell would he?"

Kat shrugged and reached for me. I laid the pillow in her lap and flopped onto it. She laughed at my dramatics and began a braid in my long hair. "My sweet summer child, you are not the same person you were then. You know that."

"I just wish I could lobotomize that part of my life out of my brain. He's such a good dude. And I was desperate. I don't even know why, now."

"I do. You were younger and dumber and he was hot and famous."

I chuckled. "True."

"Remember the way I acted with Shaun?"

"You were a mess. But that was a lot his fault."

"True."

I was silent for a minute, contemplative. I sighed and looked up at her. "I never meant to be a villain."

"No one does."

We sat that way for a few more moments, the exhaustion creeping into my limbs. The buzz of my show--the audience, the adrenaline--was wearing off and I was ready to crawl into bed. I could tell Kat was, too.

From the hallway, my phone pinged in my bag.

"Shit, I forgot to call my dad." I straightened up and headed for the door.

"Tell Kevin good night from me," Kat said from the floor.

I turned and smiled at her. "Thanks for letting me have a moment about a relationship that ended a thousand years ago."

She stood up and stretched. "Always. 'Night, Paige."

"'Night, Kat."

If you asked my father, he would have told you that I have always been a little over-dramatic. I have a tendency toward hyperbole in any situation. But when I don't text or call him the second I enter my apartment after a show, he worries. Then he panics.

So I get it from somewhere.

I quickly typed out a response to let him know I was okay and threw my heavy bag over my shoulder. My back still ached a little, but the stretching and pain reliever had helped.

The light from the street peeked through the curtains in my room, and I lit candles in lieu of the large overhead light. This tiny square of space in Astoria, Queens, was my haven. It was quiet, and the blue walls and minimal décor always made me feel calm. Kat had found this apartment, somewhat miraculously. One flyer on one streetlight pole that she just happened to pass. An older woman owned the brownstone and just wanted "a pair of nice young ladies" to move in. While the "nice" and "ladies" description of both Kat and me could be debated, she liked us enough to rent it to us on the spot.

She hadn't raised our rent in three years. For a couple of performers, it was a godsend. I feared the day Kat found a partner and decided to move out. She and I click. We met in a jazz class downtown and bonded over a shared hatred of fouettés and that we were wearing the same leotard. It was a natural progression to meeting for coffee, then drinks and dancing, then texting constantly, then deciding to move in together.

My three older brothers were some of my favorite people, but Kat was the sister I had always wanted. And she always listened to me, even when I was being as dramatic as my dad accused me of being.

Especially with Ethan.

Whenever I thought about the way I'd behaved with Ethan during our relationship and then when he found someone to love, deep, burning shame punched me in the gut. It was just one of those relationships--he was one of those people, really--that makes you completely crazy. You'd do anything to hold onto them but also feel like you don't deserve them. That's what Ethan was to me.

Broadway star Ethan Carter. Cinnamon roll Ethan Carter. Broadway's favorite boy, Ethan Carter. Tall and blond and real and kind, his incredible talent impossible to ignore. He was mine, for a while.

I pulled out my water bottle and sipped as I gazed out of my window. *Might as well feel it all now, or I won't be able to sleep.* I unearthed the Ethan Memory Box from deep within the recesses of my brain and played them like a movie in my mind.

We met auditioning. He was going in for a lead, called in by the producers and director. He rarely had to beg for an audition. I was clawing my way through the union Equity audition calls every day, just trying to get in the ensemble of a show, any show. Hell, I would have done a revival of the reviled *Taboo* if that were offered to me. I just wanted to be onstage. Right after college, I'd gotten cast in a tour of *Rent* which I thought would launch me into a successful career, but it doesn't always work that way. After a year of touring, I did a few off-off-Broadway things. They went nowhere, but the tour and those shows beefed up my resume. Or so I thought.

After yet another dance call, yet another number, yet another probable rejection, I stood outside the building unsure of what to do with the rest of my day--and life-- when the door opened behind me.

And there he was. He'd smiled at me, that famous smile that made you feel like you were the only person in the world, the only person who mattered. He obviously felt the opposite of what I was feeling. His audition must have gone well.

And that was it. For some reason, that beautiful man wanted me to go to lunch with him. Wanted me to be with him. He was so reassuring about my audition, convincing me that maybe this time was the one. We were inseparable for a couple of months. I was completely thrilled and loved every second, but I kept getting rejection after rejection after rejection. And I started to be...

Well.

A little ridiculous.

He didn't deserve the way I'd treated him. I was having trouble watching his career take off, seeing his sold-out shows full of screaming girls. The stage, television, and indie movie contracts. I wanted to keep him around because he was so wonderful to me. But I also felt that I didn't deserve him, that he deserved someone on his level. So I would pull a disappearing act like it was some kind of test. As the months went on, there were times I wouldn't answer him for days, knowing he'd be getting desperate. Then I'd show up and pretend like I hadn't been gone.

My life, meanwhile, felt like it was careening in the opposite direction. The bartending I had been doing to sustain myself was taking its toll on me. Every day, I would spend hours in line for Equity calls, and every night, hours behind the bar. And all the while, Ethan was having success after success and still claiming he loved a loser like me.

He didn't call me a loser, of course. I did.

In fact, he got really angry when I got down on myself. I would never forget when he'd exploded at me one evening, the angriest I'd ever seen him get. And of course, somehow, it was positive anger.

Golden boy Ethan Carter.

"Paige," he'd yelled, exasperated after I'd spent another hour decrying my efforts and the industry and why I couldn't get ahead. "You are one of the most talented women I have ever met! I've seen you dance. I've heard you sing. I've read opposite you. It will come. You will get there, I promise! And then you and I..."

I'd been staring away from him, feeling shamed. I'd turned and met his eyes.

"You and I," he'd said, while wrapping his arms around me, "we'll be Broadway's power couple. No stopping us, baby."

This hadn't made a lot of sense. The biggest fight we'd had was about how he wouldn't go public about me. In the beginning, I'd agreed that we could keep it on the downlow. I understood that. But when we got more serious, he absolutely refused.

He'd wanted to keep our relationship private, wouldn't post on Instagram or Twitter about me. I had known it was stupid, but I wanted him to. I wanted him to tell the world about me.

We'd been together off and on for nearly a year. He'd tried to tell me why, something about a stalker and how he didn't want me to be hurt, but I'd ignored that. I could understand that it was scary, but I'd thought a second stalker was unlikely.

I hadn't been very nice about it, because it hurt my feelings that he didn't want to talk about me in public. I didn't think it was fair. I mean, here was this man who said he loved me, but he wouldn't tell it to the world? I didn't get it. It made me feel small, like he wasn't proud of me, like he didn't think as much of me as he said he did.

My self-esteem had plummeted.

Still, I'd hung on to him, wanting to believe. Wanting to think that he would want to say something about us once I was a Broadway actor, too. Maybe that's what it would have taken.

But the day after he'd blown up at me, it all came crumbling down.

I'd gotten another rejection, but this time, it had been something big. I had gone through seven auditions and soul-crushing nerves for a small role in a new musical. It was down to me and another girl.

They'd picked her.

Completely devastated, I'd cut everyone off but Kat, and that included Ethan. He called and texted every day, numerous times, knowing what had happened. But I couldn't face him, not after he'd expressed such confidence in me and my career just hours before.

I was wrecked. I called in sick to the bar, I cancelled another few auditions that I just couldn't face. I stayed in bed and cried and felt worthless. I considered moving back to Wisconsin. I don't know why this had been the blow to make me feel this way, but I felt everything falling apart, and my golden boyfriend was only getting wins. I didn't know how to face him. I just didn't.

I couldn't.

After a week of despair, I got a call from my agent. And this time, it was finally good news. I was in the ensemble of the Broadway revival of *Cabaret*, which I'd auditioned for months ago and forgotten about entirely.

I'd gotten a part.

Suddenly, everything was clear again. Elated, I had hastened over to Ethan's in his favorite lingerie and sundress and we'd made love, by way of apology. I didn't even apologize for disappearing. I'd only asked if he'd missed me, told him the good news, and took off my dress.

Afterwards, feeling glowy, I had started to daydream about what this would mean for us. I thought this had been what he needed to go public about me, that maybe he could see us walking the red carpet at the Tonys, too.

He'd exploded, and this time, it hadn't been positive anger.

He threw me out, accusing me of not listening to him, of going against his wishes.

That was it. He wouldn't answer me after that.

It was another blow. But I threw myself into rehearsals and tried to let him go. After a few months, I thought I could reach out and we could be friends, but that wasn't about to happen. He was furious, and it was over.

And then suddenly, there was this new girl in his life, seemingly the opposite of me.

I hated it. I hated that I had ruined our relationship, that I couldn't calm down enough to just respect what he needed to feel safe, to feel that I was safe. And I could feel a monster growing inside me when I saw her photo with him on the internet. That she got his smile directed at her...

I felt crazed. I saw red. I wasn't thinking. The fact that he wouldn't say a word about me, but all of the sudden, seemingly didn't care that he was with this girl all over the internet?

After *one day*?

Fury overtook me. I had always had a jealous streak, and it reared its ugly head with a vengeance. And so, knowing he wanted to be private, and to be honest, goaded by Kat, I thought I could make him see me again at this fancy gala.

When I'd finally found him, I had never seen his eyes so cold.

It was painful. And I did something so vindictive, I can't believe it was actually me that did it.

I posted a photo of the two of them on Twitter, and through mutual friends, I knew that it had affected them. I had hurt them both.

And I was so, so sorry.

TWO

Maybe I should have told Kat not to tell me about Ethan, no matter what she heard. It was nearly two years later, and I was better off without him anyway. Our personalities had never meshed, not really. And clearly, he'd found the one. He and Evie had been together ever since.

I didn't like thinking about that time in my life. I didn't like trying to justify the way I treated him, but maybe it was just as well. I had seen how far I would go to get "justice." Shocking myself, I could have put their lives in danger. And once I'd gotten onto Broadway and learned about the fervor of the fans...

I'm not a villain.

I watched a few neighbors return home after a late night. I had lost track of time mulling over my past behavior, and physically shook it off. To distract myself, I found the podcast Kat had been listening to and played it. Alexandra was very funny, and I couldn't get over how pleasing her voice was to listen to.

In the candlelight, I stripped off my post-show clothes and put on my fluffy bathrobe. I ran a hairbrush through my hair, then I headed to the bathroom. Over the sink, I used a cloth to wipe the thick show makeup off of my face. The podcast ended as I turned on the hot water. Alex, as she liked to be called, was incredibly charming, and I was going to look up more of her work. I turned on some music.

Under the hot water, I listened to "Hold On" from *The Secret Garden*, one of my very favorite musicals. A thought floated toward me as I hummed along.

I was so, unendingly, heart-crushingly lonely.

It's nearly impossible to date when your job is to be onstage during prime dating hours. Eight shows a week, I threw my body around the stage in an ensemble, a job so physical it left me exhausted. I couldn't fathom trying to meet up with someone after. And before a show, I couldn't have a drink, and it would be weird hours anyway. Our call time was 6:30 p.m. We're performers, so our schedules are hard to understand. We're night owls, so we can't be pinned down for normal dates.

The only people it was logistically feasible to date were other actors, and that seemed impossible, too. I had tried. There had been guys I went on dates with that went nowhere, or somewhere for a little while, or somewhere for far longer than it should have.

It had been so long since I'd felt a spark with anyone. I was so focused on my career--the auditioning, the prepping, the classes, and then the time-consuming, all-exhausting job itself--that it always seemed like bad timing.

New York City had always been my dream, and I had been there for over a decade. I moved here to attend the American Musical and Dramatic Academy, the complete opposite of the rest of my family. I came from a working class, small town Wisconsin family. They had seen how hard I had worked my whole life and supported me every step of the way. My dad and brothers drove me to classes and were in the front row of every show.

But when I got accepted to AMDA, they weren't as on board. New York was too far away and too dangerous. But I headed to the big city by myself anyway. Three bucks, two bags, one me. They came around eventually. My dad even loved to visit. But if I was honest with myself, I had always felt lonely in the city of eight million people.

With my mind on how far I'd come but how little I felt that I had accomplished, I turned off the shower, brushed my teeth and collapsed onto my bed, hair still wet and heart still hurting.

§

Loud trilling next to my face sent my heart pounding straight out of a deep sleep. Due to my phone settings, this could only mean two things: my agent was calling with good news, or my dad was calling with bad news.

And I had been really looking forward to sleeping in on my Monday off.

"This's Paige," I slurred blearily.

"Paige, I'm going to need you to wake up, and fast." Nathan, my agent. As it did every time he called, whether I wanted it to or not, hope bloomed in my chest. I sat up quickly and swished my hand down my face.

"I'm awake, I'm here. Alert and ready for duty, your honor."

Nathan snorted at my attempted alertness, but his voice was full of warmth. "I appreciate your enthusiasm."

I knew this tone. I sat up straighter. "Something good happened."

"Why else would I be calling you at eight in the morning on your day off?"

"Rip off the Band-Aid, please." My fist was clenched in my comforter.

Not everyone got along with their agents as well as I did with Nathan. He fought for me every step of the way and truly believed in my career, and not just because he'd make money from it, too. Having him and his well-respected reputation on my side for the past seven years had been invaluable. He always went above and beyond for me.

"Sister, you're going to love this." There was a smile in his voice as he dangled this carrot.

I groaned. "You're killin' me."

"Okay, short version: New musical. Pre-Broadway run in Chicago. You're up."

I think I was silent for a full minute. Nathan was patient while I wrapped my mind around this. "What's the part?" I barely dared to breathe.

"Baby, it's the lead. And you're on the short list."

This amount of confidence was unprecedented. I swung my legs over the side of my bed and rested my elbows on my knees. My hands were shaking.

"The lead." My tone betrayed my skepticism.

"Short list."

"Short list," I whispered. "How many others?"

"Three."

I blew out the breath I'd been holding and flopped back onto the bed. "So to recap: you're telling me that I am going up for the lead in a new musical, the pre-run is in Chicago, and I have a one in four chance of getting it?"

"That's what I'm telling you."

"Nathan, I'm going to puke."

I could almost hear his eyeroll. "You're fine. You'll blow them away. The first audition is on Friday and they're looking to move pretty quickly. The workshop begins in April in Chicago, since they're trying to pull a lot of talent from there. I'm going to let you process this and send over the sides and music. Call me after you read them, okay?"

"You got it. And Nathan... Thank you."

"You don't have the part yet. But I always told you. Didn't I always tell you?"

I smiled to myself. "You did."

"Talk to you soon. And I don't think I need to mention that this is fully confidential."

"So rumors will be flying any minute now."

"Precisely. But do try to keep it to yourself." There was a huge grin on his face, I knew.

"Will do." We hung up. I locked my phone, tossed it aside, and squealed, pounding my feet on the floor.

Five minutes later, I had printed the music and sides to the scenes I had to prepare and was thumbing through them in our small kitchenette. The part was perfect. I'd be playing a princess looking for love, but so much more than that. I didn't have much information by way of story, but it seemed to start out as a very normal fairy-tale- romance musical and then turned into something else entirely by the end of Act One. My character would be wronged somehow and would channel that energy into a women-led system of empowerment by the middle of Act Two. The ending was set, as far as a yet-to-be-workshopped musical could set one. She would fall in love with what she really needed in the first place: her sisterhood.

This was exactly what *I* needed.

"Mornin'." An hour later, Kat stifled a huge yawn as she went for the coffee carafe.

I couldn't contain my grin. "It is, isn't it?"

She sipped from her mug. "No ma'am, we are not doing enthusiasm on our day off. I thought you'd be a little down after..." She fell gracefully in the chair opposite mine, every bit the elegant ballerina, even this early in the morning. "Well. Today is a day for loafing."

I sat forward, desperate to share. "I can't loaf today. I have an audition to prepare for."

Kat perked up, and I found myself once again very grateful that we came from different worlds. A prima ballerina and a musical theater actor don't compete for the same roles, and that was such a blessing. It was easy to be happy for each other when we weren't also secretly envious.

"What is it?" She slid the sheet music toward her.

"New musical, and I'm up for the lead." I couldn't contain my glee, even though there was no guarantee I was going to get the part.

Kat set her coffee mug on the table, letting it sink in. Finally she whooped with joy. "*Girl.* We knew this day was coming!" She threw her arms around me and then picked up the music. "What is it?"

"Unclear but it seems really woman-powered. Princess-turned-vigilante-activist, maybe?"

"I. Am. In."

I left out the part about me moving to Chicago if I got it. We'd cross that bridge when we came to it.

"So I'm going to spend most of today shoving this in my brain," I said.

"Then you'll need brain food and to relax later. Let's order noodles and watch stupid movies tonight."

"It's a date."

She kissed the top of my head and picked up her coffee mug. As she glided out of the kitchen, she pumped her fist in the air. "That's my *girl*."

My heart was filled with love for her. There is nothing like a supportive best friend to get you through a darkness in your soul, and to share the good moments with.

§

"Thanks, Joss. See you tomorrow." I hung up my phone, a voice lesson scheduled, and the last thing on my to-do list complete. Kat uncovered our takeaway ramen and cued up *Dumb and Dumber*.

"Oh, you meant *really* stupid movies tonight," I said.

"I don't play. Sit. Eat. Decompress."

I knew she could see that my nerves were starting to get to me. The aftermath of Nathan's good news and the excitement of going up for the role had faded, replaced with the ever-present hum of anxiety I got before every audition. And the rumor mill began flying, of course. Broadway is a laughably small community, and any attempt at a closed audition process would be for naught, no matter what. I'd gotten texts all day from my friends but kept my promise to Nathan. I stayed mum. However, I now knew at least two of the three other women going up against me. And they were good.

Really good.

One had already originated a role and been nominated for a Tony. Another, Jazzy Summers, had had Broadway leads since she was a fifteen-year-old and never stopped. She was a true powerhouse. And I'm sure the mysterious third was just as seasoned. I had no idea why I'd been chosen to be in this elite group. I was just in the ensemble of my first Broadway show. I didn't have many credits besides the *Rent* tour, a few off-Broadway things and the requisite *Law & Order: SVU* episode. I wasn't even the victim or the killer, just a receptionist at the killer's office.

I made a mental note to ask Nathan if he had any idea why they had called me in for this. Was it a mistake? A cruel joke? I was nervous it was maybe both.

"Paige," I heard Kat say.

I shook my head and realized I'd been standing, staring down at my spicy miso ramen in a total daze.

She pulled me down beside her on the couch and I tucked my legs under myself.

"I know you're nervous, but you were called in for a reason, and they're going to love you."

"Yeah! I'm really lovable." I was feigning confidence.

"And you're talented. So woman up! Eat your ramen and let's watch these idiots ride a scooter to Colorado."

I snickered as she pressed play. Jim Carrey being foolish was exactly what I needed, and the spicy noodles cleared my head.

§

"Paige Parker?"

I looked up from the sides I was staring at blankly, my nerves on edge. While I was screaming on the inside, I gave the short blonde woman a beatific smile. "That's me."

"Right this way, they'll see you now."

"Thank you."

I put my bag over my shoulder and followed her into the studio. I smiled over at the pianist and then my gaze fell on the table of the producers, director, and various other production staff. They were lined up in front of the vast window from which a breathtaking view of Midtown could be seen. My heels echoed in the silent room as some of them smiled at me and some of them pursed their lips. A few weren't even paying attention to my entrance, just staring down at the various scripts, headshots, open laptops, and notes that scattered the table. One man with a slight build and wild brown curls, seemed to refuse to look at me.

It was one of the most intimidating moments of my life.

Given what I knew of the character arc, I had chosen a chaste high-necked blouse paired with a leather mini-skirt and knee- high boots. Girly and badass. I felt powerful. I felt prepared.

I felt like I was going to puke.

But instead, I smiled and set my bag down on a chair off to the side. I strode to the middle of the room and turned to face them all.

"Hello, my name is Paige Parker and I'm reading for the part of Cassandra."

"Great to see you, Paige," a bald man in a smart blazer said. "We're looking forward to seeing what you have for us."

"Why don't we start with the music first?" A woman in black-rimmed glasses too big for her face leaned forward, the rings on her fingers glinting as she folded them under her chin. This was Andrea Arroyo, a total legend, and the director.

I pretended that everything inside of me wasn't roiling and stepped into Cassandra's mind. Everything I was about to do had to project confidence. "Sounds great." I nodded at the pianist and he gave me an encouraging smile. That was nice.

I sang through the bars they'd assigned and felt amazing. My voice was strong and clear and decisive, exactly what the song called for. It was the titular ballad, where Cassandra decides to live her life on her own terms. My confidence rose, like Cassandra's did in the music, and I turned to the panel.

"That was very nice, Paige. Could you do that again? Any notes, anyone?" Andrea said.

Everyone shook their heads. At the end of the table, I noticed the man who had refused to look at me when I walked in. His expression betrayed him.

He liked me. He saw me in this part. I knew it the second he met my eyes with his.

I sang through the bars again, and I read through the sides with the bald man reading opposite me. The sides were from the beginning of the musical. Cassandra was innocent here, playful and silly, before her world comes crashing down.

I nailed it.

I met the eyes of the man at the end of the table again. He gave the slightest nod. It was all I could do not to beam right at him. But I kept it professional.

Leaving the room, I felt almost certain that this part was mine, something I almost never let myself feel. Now I knew I would agonize until I heard from Nathan, which could be days later.

But I only had to wait two hours. "Paige, they absolutely loved you. They want you back next Tuesday." Nathan was more excited than I had ever heard him.

I had to sit down on the steps of a brownstone I was passing. I took several gulps of air before I could speak.

"I'm unwell, Nathan."

"You're fine. I'm sending you new material. Let me know what you think."

"I'm stunned."

"You're not."

He was right, a little. I had asked him why on earth I was in this group of incredible performers, and he'd told me, unofficially, just what he'd heard through the grapevine: that the writer and composer, Toby Anderson, had asked for me after seeing *Cabaret*. He said that Toby couldn't keep his eyes off of me every time I was onstage. He'd pushed everyone on the production side to bring me in. I knew I was fighting an uphill battle, but I had a really good ally in it.

And a battle it was. Seven callbacks, three chemistry reads with several others auditioning for various other roles--including Dev, one of my *Cabaret* castmates--followed. I was given a slew of changes to the material as the process wore on. I could barely keep up. It was a true whirlwind.

After nearly three months, Nathan finally called while I was in Soho, shopping with Kat. By now, I had had to come clean and tell her the pre-Broadway run was in Chicago, and while we were both sad, she was totally understanding about it. I answered Nathan's call.

"Well, Paige, it looks like you won't be renewing your contract."

I stopped in the middle of the crosswalk, heart beating wildly, desperate to hear the words. "Tell me."

Nathan took a deep breath, and with unmistakable glee, said, "You got the part."

They could probably hear my screams of delight all the way up on 42nd Street.

THREE

Chicago was magical. The move went smoothly with only a few bumps along the way. My moving truck arrived a day late so I slept on the couch of one of my new castmates, Steph, cementing our friendship and providing me with an ally going into the rehearsal process. Kat had been beautifully understanding, but our goodbye was hard. She was going to have a new addition to the American Ballet sublet my room while I was gone. I was going to miss her counsel every night, about everything.

My dad was over the moon when I told him I was going to be moving three hours away from him.

"Little one," he'd said over the phone when I'd told him, using the nickname he'd given me when he knew I was going to be the last kid in his line, "this is the best news I've heard in years." His voice was thick with emotion, something that rarely happened. He was often gruff, my dad, but he had a heart of gold. I knew that he had missed me, but not just how much. It was going to be wonderful to be closer to him.

I had spent some time in Chicago in my youth, but never enough to really experience the city. Now that I'd been there for a week, in a tiny furnished studio in a Northside neighborhood written into my contract, I was falling head over heels for this magnificent town.

It was a new chapter for me. I had decided before I left New York to let Chicago be a new starting point: to stop chasing love and unavailable men, to dig into who I was and who I wanted to be. So far, I'd thrown myself into rehearsals with an incredible group of people. Some of them I had known in New York and some of them were getting their break with this show.

Including me. Taking on Cassandra was challenging and scary and wonderful. I loved what the show was shaping up to be, and being a part of the workshopping process was an education in itself. Watching the creative team work, giving them my input when asked, and having the encouragement from Toby, the composer, and Andrea, the director... It all seemed like a dream. Like I was on a TV show.

Chicago was clearing my head. I was exactly where I wanted to be.

And then ten thousand things changed.

"Come on, gorgeous, you owe me about a hundred rounds!" Dev called from across the bar. My dance partner and one of my closest friends in *Cabaret* had also been cast in the Chicago workshop, yet to be named. I smiled, pulled off my scarf, and made my way over to him.

"I owe you a lot." I planted a kiss on his cheek and signaled for the bartender. Dev had been integral in making Chicago feel like home. He was from a northern suburb and had plenty of friends in the city. He'd gathered our cast close and made sure everyone felt welcome here, in the way only Midwesterners can. We were, once again, gathered at a bar, with the weekend stretching gloriously ahead of us after a long first week of rehearsal.

"Cash only," the bearded bartender said before I ordered.

"You got it," I said and plonked a twenty down on the bar. "Two shots of MALÖRT, please."

Dev grimaced at this, knowing that I was only ordering the fiery-bordering-on-disgusting liqueur because I was in Chicago, and not because it was anything one should put in their body. The bartender raised his eyebrows and filled two shot glasses. He slid them toward us and we clinked them together, and then downed the shots. After wincing as the burning liquid made its way down, I turned to take in the scene at The Old Town Ale House.

Located across from Piper's Alley, where Second City plays, the bar is always full of performers of all types. Actors, comedians, improvisors, writers. It's small and dim and sticky and raucous and perfect. It felt like a place to call home, even if it was cash only.

The door opened, letting in the chill April air, and in walked a petite woman with a short, blonde haircut. She wore a bomber jacket over a plaid shirt and looked left and right before a smile beamed over her face... and right at me.

A fire flared in my heart. She walked toward me with a purpose and I felt my hands start to sweat. As she got closer, I took in her pixie-like features, her big brown eyes. Her killer smile. I felt a shaky grin cross my face and wondered what was happening in my body and brain.

And then she walked right past me.

"Alex! Hey!" I heard from behind me. "Great to see you!"

Oh my god, of course she wasn't smiling at me.

What on earth had just happened?

"Um, Paige?" Dev said.

I looked over to him. "Yuh..."

"Are you with us?" His grin was wide, and I knew that he'd seen my emotions all over my face.

"Right here." I glanced over to where Alex now sat with a group of folks near our friends.

"What is going on here?" He still had an impish look on his face.

I shook my head. "Nothing. Let's get a cocktail and go sit down."

After we ordered and I paid again, Dev and I sat on the rickety wooden chairs with our friends. I positioned myself so that I would be in Alex's line of vision. Dev looked from me to her and back again.

"That's Alexandra Tate. She's a comedian."

I slapped my hand to my forehead. The comedian from that podcast I had listened to all those months ago. The one I had listened to twice. "Oh? Is she funny?" I was going for nonchalant, but it came out in a squeak.

The look he gave me could have withered a flower. "Are you crushing?"

"I am not crushing. Remember? I'm not here to crush. There will be no crushing."

He nodded. "You're crushing."

"Also, I'm not gay." I swiped his arm.

"Sure, me neither." Dev took a pointed sip of his cocktail, looking me right in the eye. Dev identified as pan, meaning he liked who he liked, no matter who they were.

"Hush."

"Fine. I'll drop it. But if I need to play wingperson, just let me know."

Ignoring him, I turned to Steph, the castmate who had let me sleep on her couch, and asked her about her on-again-off-again producer lover. There was always a good story--and distraction-- there. As Steph went on about the guy who promised he would invest in anything she set out to do but never actually did, I felt the hairs on the back of my neck stand up.

Averting my gaze from Steph's riveting tale, I stole a look at Alex.

She was looking right at me. And she gave me that dazzling smile. My heart thrummed and a tingle ran up from my toes to the top of my head.

She was... Well, she was gorgeous.

Steph followed my gaze. "Oh my god, Allie?" she exclaimed.

Alex wrinkled her nose adorably and peered at Steph's face. "Steph? Is that you?"

The voice from the podcast, that husky timbre. I would have recognized it anywhere. My heart hammered in my chest and my body turned warm, whether from the shot or this lovely woman sitting in front of me. A flush crept into my cheeks.

The two seemingly old friends stood and hugged each other. Alex sat down across from Steph and me with what appeared to be a gin and tonic sweating in her hands. Dev poked me in my side.

"Stop it," I hissed at him.

"Guys, this is Alli--Alex," Steph said. "We went to high school together."

"I was Allie when I thought I was straight," Alex said, which made all of us chuckle. "I go by Alexandra Tate when I'm doing stand-up, but you can call me any variation thereof. Except Allie. I was never really an Allie."

I don't know why, but I agreed. She was definitely not an Allie. "I'm Paige," I said, tipping my glass in her direction.

"Nice to meet you." She did the same.

"You, too." Our gazes locked and I felt a shift in the atmosphere, like everything started to sparkle.

"And I'm Dev," Dev interrupted, nudging me under the table. I kicked him back.

Alex cleared her throat and smiled at him. "Hi, Dev."

The impish expression stole over his refined features again. "Oh, Steph, come get me another drink, I have a question about rehearsing... something."

Absolutely transparent, Dev. Thanks. I kicked him again and he gave me a devilish smile, pulling a mystified Steph up and toward the bar. She glanced back quizzically. All I could do was shrug as if to say *Dev is gonna Dev.*

I turned back to Alex, who was staring after the two of them with interest, one finger gliding over the rim of her glass. "I guess she didn't want to reminisce about high school."

"Does anyone?" I replied as I tried to reign in whatever was happening to me.

She turned to me and chuckled. "Absolutely not. So, Paige, what are you rehearsing for?" She placed her elbows on the tiny round table and leaned over it, her eyes bright, as if what I was about to say was the most interesting thing in the world.

I was captivated.

"A new musical, title still TBD. But they better find one quick because we open in October."

"That's so cool. I've never done a musical, can't sing for shit. But I can tell jokes, which is what I do."

That was nice to hear. Some people think of musical theater as frivolous, and it was nice that she was immediately onboard. I felt a zing in my chest, a fizz of energy. "*That's* so cool. Definitely not in my wheelhouse."

"So we've established that we're both really cool."

"Yup." We gazed at each other for a long beat. Her eyes sparkled at me and I let a smile spread across my face.

"When did you start doing stand-up?"

"A few years ago. I just got up during an open mic night and riffed on being gay in a hippie family and how my coming out wasn't so much a bang as a whimper. Which turned into sex jokes, which, let me tell you, did *not* get laughs."

That got a laugh out of me, though. "Why not?"

"I wasn't funny yet! Just being the funny friend or the class clown does not a stand-up make. So I took some classes and refined some things, and it took a while, but I just got off a tour opening for Riley Markus."

"I love her! No joke, my friends and I quote her first comedy special all the time."

Alex's eyebrows shot up. I don't think she expected me to know a relatively obscure comedian. She looked at me with such naked desire that I sat back in my chair. "Not to be condescending, but I can't believe you know who she is."

"I would watch Friday night stand-up on Comedy Central all the time in college. I fell in love with her then." Those words certainly piqued Alex's interest. The air was charged, electric. I think she liked me.

And I had no idea what I was going to do about that. Because I was not *not* interested in her.

After a few loaded moments of silence, Alex said, "So what part do you play in this new musical?"

"Her name is Cassandra." I looked down into my glass, a small smile playing on my lips, still humbled by what I was about to say next. "She's the lead."

Alex's eyes went wide and she sat back in her chair as if a strong gust of wind blew her back. "You're the lead?"

I nodded, feeling my cheeks flush even more.

"That's a huge deal!"

Still smiling, I shook my head, not used to this kind of attention. "You know what? It is! I've worked really hard for years, and this is my first lead. Getting the chance to originate a role is incredible. It doesn't guarantee that I'll be in the Broadway run. Hell, this doesn't guarantee there will *be* a Broadway run. But it's pretty much the best thing that ever happened to me."

Alex put her hand on my arm. The electricity zinging through me since she sat down became a lightning strike, her touch warming my body all over. I almost couldn't hear what she said next. "Paige, you fascinate me. Can we be those annoying people at the bar who talk until closing?"

I glanced down at her hand, my mind whirring.

This gorgeous woman was flirting with me.

I was not gay.

But I felt an instant connection to her, and I wanted to explore what that meant. And I loved how straightforward she was. I searched her warm brown eyes.

"I am so down for being those people."

Her dazzling smile hit me again, so that's exactly what we did.

Alex had grown up in the south suburbs of Chicago, and she wasn't kidding about her hippie family. Her parents, who'd decided to have her later in life, had been at Woodstock, the March on Washington, and just about every other historical event from the sixties and seventies. They hadn't let the eighties peel them away from their ideals, either. Her mom was a rather successful artist, dealing mostly in sculpture, and her dad became a lawyer for the ACLU. They brought her to her first protests against the Iraq War in the early 2000s. And when she realized she was a lesbian and came out, her parents threw her a party.

I was fascinated by this, and I told her how differently we'd grown up. My small-town Wisconsin upbringing couldn't have been more opposite. When I was only eighteen months old, my mom passed away suddenly, an aneurysm. My dad, a wonderful man, raised my brothers and me to be hard workers and truth tellers. All of them loved me fiercely and were in the front row whenever possible when I was onstage.

But my dad never talked about politics, and certainly wasn't an activist like Alex's parents. We voted when there was an election and that was that. My family just kept themselves to themselves and didn't really think about it. It wasn't until I moved to New York that I had become more politically active.

Alex seemed to enjoy listening to my journey. She was very attentive, rarely breaking eye contact, asking follow-up questions. Her eyes were kind and her empathy emanated off of her.

And she kept touching me.

I was flirting with her. And not just in a this-might-be-my- new-best-friend way. In an I-am-interested-and-find-you-very- attractive way. As she told me a story about her college improv troupe, her hand found its way to mine on the top of the table. She placed her index finger on mine and met my eyes. Almost imperceptibly, she moved her finger down. Her touch was soft but electrifying. Then she took her hand away. I missed it immediately.

I scooted my chair closer to the tiny table, touching Alex's knees with my own. "It's almost one in the morning."

"Getting late," she said softly, but I was close enough to hear. We'd both had a couple more drinks, and I was feeling sleepy but thrilled by her presence. I really didn't want the night to end.

"Little bit." I put my elbows on the table and clasped my hands around my nearly empty glass. Alex gazed at me curiously for a moment. I felt my heart beat a little faster at her attention. Seeming to make a decision, she reached over and took one of my hands from the glass and held it in her own, running her thumb along my palm. There was a jolt in my stomach as I felt tingles go all the way up my arm to my heart. Her grip was firm, steady but soft.

"Long lifeline," she said. I knitted my eyebrows together, not quite understanding.

"I told you, hippie upbringing. Your lifeline is long and you're going to be very happy."

She turned her gaze upward from my palm. I gazed into her eyes, my breathing deepening.

Then I heard myself saying, "I should go."

She startled and dropped my hand. I could tell she was a little stung. I was, too. I didn't realize those words were going to come out of my mouth, but all of the sudden it seemed like I had a lot to process.

"Oh." She sat back. "Of course. It's late."

The spell was broken.

"But um..." I wasn't sure exactly what I was about to say. I very much wanted to see her again, but I'd also never asked a woman for her number. Luckily, Alex finished the thought for me.

"Could I get your number? Maybe we could hang sometime?"

I couldn't contain my grin. "Absolutely."

FOUR

Okay. So. This was new.

Back in my little studio, I paced around, not that there was much room for that. I had brought a minimal amount of stuff with me and the rest was back in New York. But there still wasn't much room for pacing in a five-hundred square foot space. It was quite literally a box, but kind of charming.

I had washed my face, then changed into my favorite pair of sweats and a ratty old t-shirt from a Cubs *v.* Brewers game fifteen years ago. I needed comfort while my mind whirled.

First and foremost, I'd met someone. There were several problems with that.

Number one, I had vowed Chicago would be a time to find myself and settle into who I was. I was almost thirty.

While I'd spent plenty of time single, not a lot of that time had been spent without having some sort of crush.

Number two, I was not gay. I had never identified as gay. I had never dated a woman. Though I had kissed a few, in that way women did to get a guy's attention, back in my early twenties. And my mid-twenties. And other times...

Okay. I was breathing quickly, trying to make my brain work this out without going into the over-dramatic whirlwind I felt it wanting to. I felt something bubbling inside my chest, something I wasn't sure I wanted to confront. Thoughts were nudging at the back of my mind, thoughts I hadn't had in years. Ones that I'd socked away. Or I had never seen them from where I was, having just flirted with a woman that I was absolutely, totally into after three hours chatting.

Oh boy.

My mind reeled. I felt like I was watching a film strip of my life going backwards, looking for evidence of... Of what? Of my seeming gayness?

Back back back...

Angelica. The summer after sixth grade. She wore the first red bikini I had ever seen on anyone. She was on my mind for weeks. And now I was realizing. It was a crush.

Julie. My high school best friend, who was so beautiful that I told her so all the time. We were inseparable. She was beaming at me from the passenger seat as we flew down a deserted Wisconsin back road, graduation at our backs, my move to AMDA imminent. She had taken my hand. And I remember the thrill up my spine. I remember imagining what it would be like to kiss her.

Raye. She ran lights for a dance show I was in at AMDA. I hung on to her every word. She was hilarious and whip smart, and brilliant at her job. I called her my "girl crush". I kissed her in a bar for the attention of some douchey finance guys, and the look on her face when I pulled away broke my heart. She was hurt. I'd hurt her. And I'd liked the kiss.

As I sifted through these long-forgotten memories, I was actually, literally wringing my hands. I did not know people did that in real life. I crossed to the sink and poured myself a glass of water and downed it. I slammed the glass on the counter, bracing my arms against it and breathing like I'd just run a mile.

I felt like a hardened old detective, searching through my mental files for a break in the case.

Dressing rooms. I'd been in a thousand, and all the women I'd been in them with were perfection. All those times I'd sit around in my underwear with all the other girls in the cast, laughing and talking. And noticing how long and smooth someone's legs were. I realized now that I'd been feeling envy or desire or both. All of those women, so fierce and delicate and strong and vulnerable, all of us throwing our bodies around onstage every night. The way we would cuddle in the way theater people do. We touch and carouse and are so at ease with each other. In order to be vulnerable onstage and trust each other enough to catch each other when we fall, we have to be.

Michelle. Phillipa. Liz. Robyn. Cameron. All of them swam through my thoughts, and I remembered the thrill of their touch in a different, more honest way.

I flopped onto my bed and put my palms over my eyes.

And then I thought of Christopher, my high school boyfriend. David, who I was super into my first year in New York. And Raul, the most passionate man I'd ever been with. Corey. Ben. Manny.

Ethan. I was ravenous for Ethan. And several--many-- women in my past. I hadn't really noticed, or let myself, because I was so attracted to men, too.

With a sudden clarity, I sat up.

"I'm *bi*," I said aloud. A laugh bubbled out of me, alone in this tiny room, full and loud and clear. How had I not figured it out? This whole time? This whole life? This was who I was.

"I'm bi," I said again, still chuckling. And in a deep, professorial voice, "Bisexual."

I rolled over onto my side and lost myself in giggles again. This moment felt like a wall coming down, a split in my life, everything now would be after. Like AD and BC. After dick, before... well. Dirty. I laughed harder at my little in-joke with myself.

I didn't feel a change. I just felt relief. I felt real. My breathing evened quickly when I closed my eyes and I felt myself succumb to a deep, contented sleep.

The next morning, I woke up feeling more clear-headed than I had ever been. I knew Chicago would be where I found myself, I just didn't think it would be so quick and definitive. I snuggled into my pillows and sighed happily. It's a wonderful feeling to figure out who you really are.

After a few minutes of enjoying the sunshine coming in through the one big window in my studio, I rolled over and picked up my phone. A text from Dev.

> Meet me at Yolk, 12:30. I need greasy food because you were too busy flirting to stop me last night.

I chuckled. That was Dev, not asking but demanding, and always seeing me before I did. He'd been one of my closest friends for years. We'd been through the grind together in the industry, and we leaned on each other for support. I was so impressed with his drive, and his ability to let naysayers blow right around him.

When we were cast in *Cabaret*, our friendship was cemented. Eight shows a week, we relaxed in our dressing rooms between bouts of intense dancing. It was an ensemble filled with dancers, of which Dev was the best. He was my partner in most of the show, and despite almost dropping me those months back, I trusted him with my whole life. And I knew he was the exact right person to talk to after my revelatory evening. I tossed on some clothes and hurried to the restaurant.

"Hey, sweets," he called over the din of the restaurant. I made my way through the crowded foyer and hugged Dev, unable to keep from beaming. He squeezed me back knowingly and caught my eye.

"Sorry I left you to the booze last night."

"All will be forgiven with a southwestern omelet." He nodded to the host who picked up two menus and showed us to a table in the middle of the restaurant. Everything seemed brighter this morning, the consequence of figuring something out about yourself that you'd known all along. It had just been lying dormant, waiting for me to catch up.

We sat and were brought waters and we ordered coffee. Dev gave me a mischievous look. "Look at that gorgeous man, on your six."

I turned and nodded approvingly at the man a few tables away. He was the epitome of tall, blond, and strapping, like Prince Charming. He was holding the hand of an equally attractive woman.

"And she's not bad either." His tenor was teasing and I immediately knew that he knew.

I whipped my head around to him and stared straight into his eyes. "She's gorgeous."

"I knew it," he crowed in triumph.

I felt a weight lift off of me as Dev laughed and unwrapped a straw for his water. He lifted an eyebrow at me. "So this Alex gal..."

I moved so the server could put down our coffees in front of us and added cream to mine. Slowly, I twirled my spoon in the mug, making him wait.

"*Paige.*"

I chuckled. "I like her. And yes, last night, I figured out that I'm bi."

That was easy. It always is when you're true to yourself.

"I could have told you that years ago. Remember Michelle?"

"Oh my god. Yes!" It had been when we were both dancing for a benefit concert. Michelle Lupkus was a legit Broadway legend, and she'd taken a liking to me. I was obsessed with her now that I think about it. We spent a lot of time together.

"That was a *crush*, baby."

I nodded, clarity rushing through my mind, much as it had last night. "It so was. A huge crush." I took a sip of my coffee and Dev grinned at me from across the table. "Why didn't you tell me?"

"That's not something you can tell someone. You figured it out."

"True. It took a while, but I did. Wish I had known sooner."

He reached across the table and took my hand. "But then you wouldn't be you."

I squeezed his fingers. "Another truth."

"So how do you feel?" He turned his attention to the menu briefly while I collected my thoughts. I scanned my own, barely registering the items.

"Like a mystery has been solved," I finally said.

He looked up and a huge smile crossed his face. "That's wonderful news. Let's get a mimosa to celebrate."

Ten minutes later, we drank a toast to knowing exactly who we were and ordered our omelets.

"You seem lighter. Freer."

"I hope that comes through in rehearsals. I haven't been holding anything back but knowing who I am is really going to help me find out who Cassandra is, going forward."

"Honey, you are killing it in that room. Everyone is so impressed, seriously."

"Thanks, Dev." He raised an eyebrow and stared at me expectantly. It took me a moment before I understood he was fishing for a compliment. I rolled my eyes and obliged. "You are, too. I love you as the Duke, you're so sneaky but charismatic."

"Sneaky but charismatic. Put that on my tombstone." We snickered into our champagne glasses.

Our food arrived and Dev ate greedily. I could barely touch my toast and eggs because all I could think of was Alex. Dev noticed my full plate and sat back. "So tell me about Alex. Steph spoke really highly of her. She said that she was the funniest girl in high school."

I blushed a little.

"Look at you, you *like* her."

I threw a toast point at him. "Hush. She's pretty great. We had a really fun conversation. Talked about our families and life and everything, really."

"You got deep." He munched on my tossed toast.

"We did, a bit." I bit my lip, remembering the heat of her when our knees touched under the table.

"Did you get her number?" Dev spooned jam onto his English muffin.

"She got mine."

"Are you going to date her?"

I toyed with my eggs, and then sat back. I was frustrated by my plan being thwarted, but desperate to see Alex's smile again. "The whole point of me being here was so I could find myself and be who I am on my own."

"And that happened. In like, a really huge and concrete way already, so-o-o..."

I narrowed my eyes at Dev, considering what he'd just said. That was true. I did come here to do the best job I could in the show, and to find who I really was. And he was right, that had happened in a really cemented way, really quickly. But another thing was needling the back of my mind.

"Regardless of whether we start dating, there's a finality to it. I don't actually live here. And if the gods smile upon us and the show goes to Broadway and I'm asked to go with it, what then? Alex has roots here, deep ones. So what would be the point of getting into anything serious if it's inevitable that it will end?"

"Good point, but that doesn't mean you can't have fun while you're here. She'd be the first woman you've dated, so you shouldn't put all your eggs in one basket anyway."

"Coming from you, that's a strong argument."

He wagged a finger at me. "We do not slut shame around here, missy. I was a touring artist for a long time, and it's normal to have a port in every storm."

I snickered. Good ol' Dev. "May you never change, buddy."

"Promise." He clinked his champagne glass to mine and drained his mimosa. I attempted to eat more of my toast and was interrupted by my phone beeping with a text.

> Would it be weird to ask you to brunch tomorrow? Should I wait the requisite three days?

Alex. My whole body responded. A heady feeling began in my chest and then spread all the way down to my toes and all the way out to my fingertips. I couldn't help laughing again. I finally figure out I'm bi and three seconds later, a woman asks me out.

And I was going to say yes.

Dev was staring at me from across the table, an amused expression on his face. "Alex?"

"Yes."

"Asking you out?"

"Yes."

"That's my girl." He beamed and I returned a wide smile, then typed.

> Not at all, I would love to.

Dev and I spent a bit more time chatting, before we split the bill and parted ways. As I walked home in a bit of a daze, I absentmindedly hummed to myself and realized it was "Only Us" from *Dear Evan Hansen*. What if...

Alex sent me a place and time, a diner called Mortar & Pestle that I hadn't been to before. We texted back and forth for a bit. I was thrilled at the idea of a date, a first in a while for me, and I spent the rest of Saturday trying on various clothes and discarding them for one reason or another. Nothing seemed right, but I finally settled on casual. My favorite pair of jeans, combat boots, and a green sweater I'd loved for years. The sweater made my eyes seem more hazel in the sunlight.

I hoped Alex would like the effect.

Sunday morning rolled around lazily and I made myself a cup of coffee. I took a long, leisurely bath, trying to calm my excited nerves, and got ready. My phone trilled while I was shaving my legs. My dad. I decided he could wait until later and put on my chosen outfit. Filled with nervous excitement, I walked to the brunch spot.

In the light of day, Alex was even cuter than she was in the dim bar. She was shorter than me by an inch or two, but what she lacked in height she made up in presence. It seemed like the entire restaurant, teeming with patrons, revolved around her.

Or maybe that was just me.

She looked up from her phone when I entered and it was as if time stopped for a moment. We locked eyes and a smile burst onto her face. She strode toward me as if this wasn't our first date, as if we had done this for a thousand other Sundays. Her arms wrapped around me and I returned her warm hug.

"I'm so glad we could do this," she said in that raspy tone of hers.

"Me, too." A thrill rushed through me as she swept her hands down my arms.

She smelled like strawberries, and something else, spicy but sweet. Maybe nutmeg. We disentangled ourselves and turned to the host, who led us to a sunny corner of the restaurant near the front. Everything about this place was warm: the lighting, the blonde wooden tables, the other diners who seemed happy and light.

This felt like exactly where I was meant to be.

Once at the table with fresh coffee in front of us, she laid her napkin in her lap and I did the same. I dropped my gaze, feeling suddenly shy. I could feel her looking at me, and I admired her directness.

"It's nice to see you again. I have to tell you, it's been a little while since I've been on a proper date. I'm a little nervous."

I gave a shaky laugh. "Oh thank god, me too. In fact--" I chewed my lip and turned toward the window. She propped her chin in her hands, signaling me to go on.

"I have to tell you that the reason I left so abruptly the other night is that this is my first date with a woman."

Her eyebrows went up as she took in this information. "Oh."

"Yeah. I never, um. Well, I didn't figure out I was bi until that night, actually."

She paused, and I saw uncertainty cross her features. She reached over to the sugar packets and poured half of one into her coffee. Sweet, but not too.

"You were so self-assured talking and flirting with me, though. I thought--"

"I'm very attracted to you." She made me bold, unafraid.

She looked up from her coffee, still obviously a bit concerned, but flattered. "You seem really sure about that."

"I am. This isn't a one-off thing. Flirting with you all night made me realize who I've been my whole life. It's not a phase; I've just never been out with a woman before. I wanted you to know right off."

She sat back. "Thank you for trusting me with that." It seemed she was searching for the right words. She sucked in her cheeks.

I took a sip of coffee, letting her think it through. I wanted this to go well, and I wanted to get it all out in the open before anything happened.

She peered at me. Her expression was serious, but her brown eyes were sparkling. "Are we just going to get really deep off the bat?"

"I don't see any reason why not."

Smiling, she leaned forward over the table. "I've been out for a long time. I don't know if anyone in my life considered I was straight, ever. And I'm going to be really blunt, and I hope this doesn't hurt your feelings, but I'm not interested in a project, and I'm not interested in someone who doesn't know what she wants. So if you say I can trust that you want to be on a date with me, then I will. But if you're feeling unsure, I don't want to be messed with." She paused and knitted her eyebrows together, looking down. I got the feeling she'd been in that very situation before.

"To be perfectly frank, I asked you out because I felt a connection with you for the first time in quite a while." Her eyes met mine, her smile reaching them. "It's not usually my M.O. to be so forward, but I can tell you're special, Paige." A little hesitantly, she reached her hand toward mine. I slid my fingers through hers, warm and steady. She grinned.

"I can tell you're special too. And--" I took a deep breath and spilled out the whole thought process I'd gone through after meeting her. She listened intently, nodding and laughing in all the right places. We were still holding hands when I finished. "The thing is, it's something that I easily ignored because I like men, too. But then you breezed into that bar, all adorable pixie energy, and I-- Well, here we are."

"I think that's the first time I've gotten 'adorable pixie energy.'"

I chuckled. "Well. You seem pretty magical to me."

She traced her thumb along my lifeline again and when I met her gaze, I saw blazing desire. "I'm glad you told me all of that. Thank you."

I held my breath, hoping she wasn't going to tell me we should just be friends.

"Now, are you a more savory or sweet breakfast person? Because that could be the real dealbreaker." She let go of my hand, but not my gaze, and picked up her menu. I laughed along with her.

It turned out that we were both savory breakfast people, and we swapped her eggs benedict for my spinach omelet halfway through our meal.

"So, presumably, you haven't told your family you were going out with a lady?"

I put a bite of eggs in my mouth and shook my head as I swallowed. "Not as much, no."

"Do you think, I mean, this has to go well first, but do you think they'll be cool?"

"I don't know, is this going well?" I wiggled an eyebrow at her, grinning.

She put down her fork and gave me that intense gaze again. "If it's not, I've become really bad at reading people."

I sighed, happy to hear that. "Then I don't know what they'll say. I'm sure there will be questions and an adjustment period. But yeah, I think they'll be cool."

Her expression was empathetic. "I hope you're met with as much love as I was."

"Thank you. And it's not as if..." I glanced at her, already feeling sad that what I was about to say was true. "I mean, you know, I don't live here. So..."

"And I'm probably going on tour later this summer, and I teach comedy classes here, so. This can't go anywhere."

Her bluntness was refreshing, even though I already didn't want to say goodbye. "I don't see how." My voice came out sounding sad.

Alex, however, brightened and sat up straight in her chair. "Then I propose this, Paige Parker. Let's enjoy the moment together. Let's have a fun summer. And let's make the most of the time we have together." She raised her coffee mug at me and leaned a little closer.

I picked up my own, placing my elbows on the table. Our faces were inches apart and I saw her sharp intake of breath. I gave her a mischievous grin. "As long as this date is going well."

She just returned my grin and clinked her mug on mine. As we sipped, our eyes didn't stray from one another's and I felt a deep swooping sensation through my belly.

Wow. This girl.

Alex insisted on paying the bill, and promised she'd let me get it next time. When she'd said that, we'd both beamed at each other like loons, thrilled there would be a next time. We walked out into the neighborhood, wandering past cafes and antique shops. The air was full with the promise of spring.

She took my hand and I laced my fingers through hers. We were a perfect fit.

"Do you have anything to do for the rest of the day?" she said as we ambled up the street.

"Not really. You?"

"I usually spend Sundays loafing around, recovering from the night before."

"What'd you do last night?"

"I went up at The Comedy Clubhouse, down in Wicker Park. It's a great spot. I'm working on some new material, and really hoping something big happens soon."

"Honestly, why any of us choose to be in the performance arts is a true mystery."

"Truly. If I could just get my own Netflix special. Or get in a writer's room."

"You will." I squeezed her hand.

"How do you know? You've never heard my stuff." She was teasing and bumped her shoulder into mine.

I blushed and looked up at the sky. "I may have heard you on a podcast. Or two."

She stopped short, her mouth agape as she looked at me. "What?"

"My roommate was listening to you one night, and I maybe Googled a little."

She laughed aloud and put her arm around my waist as we continued down the street. "I may have Googled a little, too. Those press photos for *Cabaret*. Yowza."

I chuckled. Yowza. What an adorable dork. "Please don't think that's what my real underwear looks like."

"Bummer." The teasing look she gave me made my heart stutter. I felt the warmth of her arm around me and realized I hadn't felt this way about anyone in a long, long time.

We passed a collie with his owners and both said *aww* at the same time. Her laughter was sultry and meshed with my more high-pitched almost-giggle in some kind of harmony.

"While I'm waiting for my dream to arrive, your dream came true. I want to know more about the show."

"I think it's going to be really good. I'm loving what they're giving me for Cassandra. She's sweet but strong, and very determined, and I'm looking forward to what they're going to do with the ending. Workshopping is so different from just rehearsing an already written show. They're asking me what I think about her storyline and interested in my input. It's so flattering and intimidating. I'm sorry, I'm jabbering."

"No, don't," she paused where we were, down a quiet side street lined with trees. She stood in front of me and softly placed her hands on my waist. "I could listen to you talk about your passion for hours."

I gazed into her warm brown eyes, feeling like a brand-new person. I put my hand on the soft skin of her cheek and caressed down her jawline. Everything seemed to sparkle again. The sun was warm on my back and the trees were just beginning to bud.

I watched her take a deep breath as she pulled me closer. My heart began to pound. I stepped closer to her and wound my fingers through the hair at the nape of her neck.

When her soft lips met mine, something inside of me exploded. Everything I'd ever known seemed to tip over an edge. I was upended. I ran my hands down her back and pulled her closer, that swooping sensation I had felt when she first touched me coursing through me in waves.

Her grip tightened around my waist as our kiss deepened. As her hands slid up my back, her tongue swirled around mine, taking my breath away. I could barely stay standing as her body pressed against mine deliciously.

I moved one hand to her waist and cupped her face in the other. I wanted to feel every part of her, and she responded by winding her fingers through my long hair and biting my bottom lip. I let out a soft groan.

Breathing heavily, she tipped her head back and searched my face. That blazing look was in her eyes again and I swear I could see everything to come, right there in that one kiss. I let a smile slowly spread across my lips and she returned it. She brushed her nose onto mine and then, light as a feather, her lips found mine again.

And then my phone trilled.

"Saved by the bell," she half-whispered. We broke apart, our hearts racing. I looked at her quizzically and she grinned playfully. "I'm just saying it's been a while since I've made out with someone on the street in the middle of a Sunday."

I snickered and retrieved my phone from my bag. As I did, the expression on her face made me feel like the only woman in the world.

My heart fell. "Aw, man. Email from the director. A few changes I need to review by tomorrow's rehearsal. Our street make-out sesh will have to wait."

"Damn. But probably for the best." She motioned across the street where a cute, young family was just leaving their apartment looking like they were on their way to a picnic.

I grinned and squeezed her waist. "Wouldn't want to scandalize the neighborhood."

She stepped closer to me with that intense look in her eyes. "Wouldn't we though?"

Before I went home to review the new pages, we certainly tried.

FIVE

"Paige?"

I started at my name and looked up at Toby. I had been fully staring off into space, barely registering the rehearsal studio. I was blind to the long wall of mirrors, the portable barres for warm-ups, the wooden blocks and fake doors that made up our set pieces for the time being, because I'd been thinking of Alex and her soft lips. "What's up?"

"Can we speak with you for a moment?"

Andrea, the director, and Toby, the composer, motioned for me to follow them to a corner of the room. My stomach instantly started doing backflips. In the ten seconds it took us to cross the studio, I thought that I would be fired, that I was doing a terrible job, that they were going to replace me, that I was worthless and talentless and they'd finally realized what a horrible mistake they had made.

I do not know how other actors got over this insecurity, always prevalent, no matter how confident you were in real life. Maybe we're all just faking it.

I did not expect what they said next. Andrea cleared her throat.

"Paige, we're so pleased with the work you're doing."

The air went out of my lungs in a whoosh. Thank god.

"And we wanted to run something by you. Now obviously, Cassandra is a goddess in her own right, and we do like the ending, when she's conquering the land. But we also wanted to include a love story--maybe just implied--with another woman. Would that be all right with you?"

I do not think they expected me to laugh in their faces. Life was certainly imitating art.

"I'm so sorry, I didn't mean to laugh, it's just--" I decided not to tell them the recent development in my personal life. Alex and her sweet pixie face was all mine for now. "That would be excellent. I would love that."

Toby's eyebrows shot up and I caught his eye. He tilted his head at me. I winked and his smile grew. "That's great, Paige. Scrap the stuff we sent you yesterday. A whole new ending is coming." He bounced away, my advocate and now my friend. Toby, I had learned, had fought tooth and nail to give me this role, and I was eternally grateful for his optimism and that I was making him proud.

"I think now that we'll have an ending he's pleased with, we'll finally have a show," Andrea told me under her breath. I smiled at her.

"I think it's going to be fantastic. Especially with you at the helm."

She looped her arm through mine, giving it an affectionate squeeze. "You got that right, sister."

I picked up my sheet music and glanced around the room. My castmates were beautiful and diverse and I felt a swell of pride at what this show would represent and who would be able to see themselves in it. Alex and I were going to see each other again later in the week, and we continuously texted each other. I was enamored with her, enamored with this new show family, enamored with Chicago, and felt like everything was perfect in my world.

Well, nearly everything. I still had no idea what to say to my dad and brothers. They were all so excited to have me nearby, and if I was honest with myself, I was avoiding them. I genuinely hadn't wanted to visit them when I'd arrived in Chicago. I had needed to settle into the city and the new routine. But it had been nearly a month, and they were getting curious as to why I hadn't made plans to visit yet.

Before I met Alex one week ago, I had planned on a weekend away soon. But now that she was in my life, I didn't want to leave. Weekends were a time we could spend together. And I still wasn't sure how to tell them I was dating a woman.

I was ruminating on this as I walked up the steps to Alex's three-flat. She lived on the top floor of a gray stone building. I rang her bell, shifting the bouquet of gardenias from one arm to the other. The door buzzed and I walked up the stairs, feeling flutters of anticipation. Brunch was one thing, but dinner in her home was quite another.

She opened the door and I immediately felt calm, just seeing her sweet, open face. For a few moments, we stood in her doorway not saying anything, just letting the air between us crackle and fizz.

"Hi," she finally said.

In lieu of a response, I put my palm to her cheek and kissed her softly. She responded immediately, pulling me inside and shutting the door, all while her lips remained on mine. We broke apart, grinning.

"Hi," I told her. She glanced down at my arms, where I cradled the slightly smushed bouquet. "These are for you."

Alex accepted them and put them immediately to her nose. "No joke, gardenias are my favorite." She peered at me from behind the flowers, her expression bright.

"Sounds like it was meant to be, then."

Another dazzling smile exploded across her face and she turned down the hallway. "Come on in, make yourself at home. Dinner is almost ready and the wine is breathing."

I followed her down the long hallway of the classic Chicago train-car apartment. The living room at the front led to the dining room, which led to the hallway and bedroom, and at the back, the kitchen. All in a row. The hallway walls were peppered with photographs of her friends and family. She was unbelievably photogenic, and in these pictures, I could see that she lived life to its fullest. Peeking into her bedroom, I saw a gray cat snoozing on her bed. It opened one eye and regarded me lazily, then shoved its face into its paws and went back to sleep.

"That's Sammy," Alex called from the kitchen, "He's going to ignore you for a while. Don't take it personally."

"I'll try not to, but cats generally love me." I entered the warm kitchen which smelled deliciously of something Italian. There was a small dinette set against the corner windows and the space was larger than I expected. Alex clearly liked to spend time in here. The kitchen was friendly and lived in, not like some of the all-white kitchens in newer condos. This was a place where love happened.

Alex poured me a glass of wine and then one for herself. She went back to fussing with something on the stove and asked how my week was. I told her about rehearsal and she told me about her day job as a virtual assistant. It sounded boring, but she was so clever that she made the tedious tasks seem interesting.

"Are you Italian?" I asked her as she bustled about.

"How'd you know? I'm half. Italian and German."

"The way you're cooking, moving around. My best friend in high school lived with her Italian grandmother. You remind me of her."

"I remind you of an old lady?" Alex's voice was full of mirth and she turned to me with a sauce covered wooden spoon. I laughed through a sip of wine and stood up.

"A very beautiful, very talented old lady."

"Taste," she demanded, looking into my eyes. My heart skipped a beat. She did something to me that I had rarely ever felt. She held up the sauce covered spoon. I took it between my lips, keeping my gaze on hers, and tasted the best tomato sauce I'd ever had in my life.

"Holy shit, Alex, that is incredible. I'm impressed."

She beamed with pride. "Thank you. As it happens, that is a little old lady's recipe. My grandmother's."

I chuckled and leaned against the counter next to the stove. "Give her my regards."

Alex looked down into the saucepan and a pensive look flickered over her face. "She passed three years ago. I miss her all the time. She was fierce and funny and always encouraged my comedy. That's why I spend so much time in here, cooking. It makes me feel close to her."

"She sounds like a very cool lady."

"She was." Alex met my eyes and a small smile formed on her lips. "And you're going to love her pasta."

Alex motioned to a beautiful array of fresh noodles next to a pasta maker on the opposite counter. "Grab those, would you?"

"I will, but I will also tell you, I am absolutely hopeless in the kitchen." I brought over the spaghetti noodles and she motioned to a pot of boiling water. I dropped them in and Alex drizzled a bit of olive oil and stirred them quickly, presumably to prevent them sticking.

"That's okay, I've got us covered."

I had moved to the table to get our wine glasses and handed hers over. "Glad to hear it." She clinked my glass and stepped closer to me. When her lips met mine, she tasted delicious.

§

"I don't think I can ever eat again. That was incredible. I can't believe you made me fresh pasta." I put down my fork and sat back contentedly. I picked up my glass and raised it. "To your grandmother."

"To Mary." Alex held my gaze as we sipped. "So how is your family? Your dad and brothers, right?"

I sighed and took in Alex's eager expression. I felt like I could tell her anything. Her warm brown eyes became concerned the longer I looked at my wine glass.

"I don't know. I mean, my dad and I have spoken this week. Of course we have but--" I didn't know how to finish this. I certainly didn't want to make Alex uncomfortable, but what was happening between us was so real, and it made me nervous. And I didn't want to scare her off by telling her that, seeing as this was our second date.

She guessed what I was feeling anyway, in a way that gave me the go-ahead to talk about it. "You mentioned that they're a little more conservative than my family."

"They are, that seems obvious. And I don't think that they would disown me or anything. I'm just unsure what their reaction would be to me dating a... You."

She chuckled. "A woman, you mean?"

I smiled wryly. "Yeah. I'm not going to not tell them I'm bi, I just don't want... I don't want judgment or animosity. I want them to love me for who I am, no matter what."

She tipped her glass in my direction. "Welcome to being queer."

I tipped mine back, grinning. "Happy to be here."

While I was trying to figure out what I was so afraid of, having no evidence that my family wouldn't accept me, Alex was one step ahead of me. I would come to realize that this happened with most things. She would almost always know what I was feeling before I did.

"Have they given you any indication, ever, that they wouldn't love you as you are?"

I shook my head. "Never."

"Then I don't think you have anything to worry about. It's just big, important news."

I tilted my head and regarded her as she relaxed in the chair opposite me. "How do you do that? How do you make everything seem so much better?"

She simply smiled softly and we gazed at each other for a long moment. She set her wine glass down and picked up my hand, while glancing down shyly.

"You know, Paige," She trailed her thumb along my palm. "I haven't stopped thinking about you all week. I keep thinking about your eyes, your laugh, your lips. I can't get you out of my head. I am completely enamored of you."

My heart skipped a beat. This is everything I'd ever wanted to hear out of a partner and I was finally hearing it. She raised her eyes to mine, and I saw that burning look there again, showing me that she wasn't bullshitting me. Every second I was with her felt like coming home. I threaded my fingers through hers and leaned closer. She brushed my nose with hers and brought her hand to my cheek.

"I really like you. I feel the same. I know it might only be for a short time, but I want to keep dating you," I said. Her confidence had inspired me and I touched my lips to hers, kissing her slowly, deeply. She tasted of sweet wine and her grandmother's sauce. I was home.

A few minutes later, I got up and stacked our two plates. She watched me as I began to fill the sink with water. "You don't have to do that," she said as she filled our wine glasses with the last of the bottle. She brought mine over. I nudged her hip with my own.

"You cook, I clean, partner."

She clinked her glass with mine. "Deal."

"As for my family, I'll figure it out. I just don't know how much to tell them right now."

"Well, that's the good thing about having a gender-neutral name. Just tell him you met someone called Alex and deal with the rest later. Because--and I hope this doesn't come as a surprise--I'm in this. Like, completely in this."

I paused with my hands in the soapy water. "Have you told your parents about me?"

"Posey could sense an energy change in me." Alex snickered a little at my expression at this revelation. "I told you, hippies."

"We really couldn't have come from more different places, could we?"

"About as different as we can get in middle America."

We chatted about our upbringings, getting to know each other better, as I washed and she dried the dinner dishes, and then we moved to the couch with the half glasses of wine.

"So Paige, you are newly queer," Alex began as she selected a movie on Netflix.

"Oh wow, I hadn't really thought about that. I guess I am."

"Well, to be fair, you figured out that you're bi, but it's not new that you are."

To be understood this way anchored me. I scooted closer to her. "True."

"On this momentous occasion, then, I must show you all of the lesbian movies that you may not have appreciated, if you've even seen them before."

I chuckled. "I'm in."

But I'm A Cheerleader, a film I had heard about but never seen, was subversive and wonderful, but also so sexy I wanted to drag Alex to her room. She seemed to feel the same way, because at the end of the film, she reached out her hand and I melted into her arms.

She cupped my chin in her hand and touched her lips to mine, light as a feather at first. Impatient, I deepened our kiss, parting her lips with my tongue, and that seemed to be all the permission she needed. A fire burned in my chest as her tongue slid along mine. I nipped at her bottom lip, then kissed along her jawline. She buried her face in my neck and trailed her tongue toward my ear. Her breath sent shivers down my spine as she whispered, "I can't get enough of you."

I gasped and caught her lips again, feeling her breath mingle with mine. I trailed my hand along her back and found my way under her shirt. She moaned softly as I marveled at her velvety skin under my fingertips. Gently, she pushed me back into the couch and I sank into the soft cushions. She gazed at me, her eyes almost black with desire, our breathing coming in gasps.

Greedily, I pulled her down to me, now running both of my hands under her shirt. I couldn't get enough of her softness. Her skin. Her lips. Her hand traced lightly down my arm and found my waist, her fingers sliding under my shirt. I inhaled sharply at the sparks flying from her fingers to my bare skin. I wrapped my legs around her, my hand on the back of her neck, our lips and tongues moving together as a brand-new passion flowed through me.

"Paige, hold on." She pulled herself up on her hands and panted above me. I looked up at her curiously, her mussed hair and dark eyes. "I don't want to do anything that makes you uncomfortable."

I raised one eyebrow at her. "Do I look uncomfortable to you?"

She smirked. "Definitely not. But I don't want to move too fast. You've never been with a woman before and I don't want to freak you out."

Her care for me emanated off of her. I felt so safe. And while I certainly wasn't a prude, this was new for me. "You're right. I think. Yeah. You're right. Let's take it slow."

She leaned down and touched her lips to mine again chastely, and then pulled me up and swung her legs over my lap.

Cuddled that way, we talked until two in the morning. I opened up to her and could feel every wall I'd had up begin to crumble. She could relate to my insecurities and fears because she had some of the same ones. And I hadn't laughed that hard in ages. Everything seemed clear to me as we said goodnight at her door. This, Alex, was what I had been waiting for my whole adult life: to feel seen and understood and to laugh so much my sides hurt.

We made plans for Sunday and kissed goodnight, sparks flying all over. I could feel myself falling right into the deep end, and I wasn't going to do anything to stop it.

"So when do I get to see you perform?" I said as I loped up the stairs to the rehearsal studio, enjoying my morning chat with Alex.

"Ooh. Well. That's a whole thing."

I waited for her to say something else. When she didn't, I said, "What does that mean?"

"Well. I'm just kind of shy about it."

I could feel my face explode into a grin. This beautiful woman, this gregarious, hysterical, amazing story-teller was afraid to let me watch her comedy set. "That is adorable."

"Arrrgh, let me think about it. I'm nervous!"

"Don't be nervous. You're hilarious. But take as much time as you need. I can't wait to catch your act."

I could picture her sitting in her underwear on her bed, Sammy purring at her side, her blonde hair mussed from sleep. Just as I'd left her. I could hear the smile in her voice. "Call you later?"

"You better."

We hung up and I entered the studio, lighter than air. It had been a month since our first date, and it didn't take long to fall into a routine together. And while there were plenty of wandering hands, we hadn't explored each other completely. But we were sleeping together most nights. I was still a little shy about going all the way with Alex. I knew what I liked in the bedroom, which could certainly be a start to pleasing her, but I was timid. She respected that completely and was happy to wait until I was ready.

Ours was the best relationship I'd ever had. Alex didn't play any games, and I never questioned her feelings for me. I never wanted her to wonder how I was feeling, either, so she knew I wanted to spend as much time as possible with her. Against all odds, I'd finally found someone who didn't make me a dramatic mess.

And when Sammy finally cuddled up next to me instead of her one night, Alex had melted and kissed me in a way that let me know she felt the same way.

I was leaving for the next weekend, however. After getting lovingly but increasingly pestered by them, I had finally relented and was visiting my family. I wasn't sure I would tell them about Alex. She and I hadn't decided we were anything serious yet, especially since our relationship did have an end date. We were still deep in this infatuation that I knew from experience would eventually fade and we would break up, or it would turn into something deeper. I hoped it was the latter.

As I dumped my bag onto a chair in the studio, my phone pinged.

> Okay okay. You're on the list. Thursday night.

I smiled down at the text. A link to Alex's next performance followed and I clicked it. She would be third out of five comedians, several of whom I'd heard of, and not just from her. I was impressed. Performing at The Laugh Factory was nothing to sneeze at. I couldn't wait to see her onstage.

I can't wait.

§

"I'm dating someone. There's no joke. I'm just bragging."

The audience laughed heartily, and mine was the loudest. I took another sip of my gin and tonic. Alex was onstage in an intimate room, commanding it like she'd been on it her whole life. She wore her favorite button-down army-green shirt, the combat boots I'd met her in, and jeans that hugged her ass in a way that made me quiver.

"We've been together a month, so obviously, we've moved in together." She took a stance and pointed at the audience, saying definitively, "Lesbians!"

She was so cute. Alex continued to joke about how fast lesbians usually moved, and how because I was bi, we were moving at half-speed.

I noticed a couple of women turn to each other with knowing smiles. They kissed lightly. Sweet.

"Wait, are you a lesbian?" Dev whispered next to me. I kicked him, something that was becoming routine.

"No, it's for the joke. I still find you unbelievably attractive."

"Obviously," he snickered. "She's hilarious."

"I know. I mean, I knew that, but this is something else entirely."

Alex told several stories about growing up with her hippie parents, her coming out party, a few past relationships that made me feel only a twinge of jealously. She respectfully didn't say anything else about us, nothing we hadn't discussed already, which left me happy but also wanting. Maybe I wanted her to talk more about our relationship. Maybe I wanted to be out in the open.

I also knew that seeing her perform so wonderfully made me want to lay her down and worship every bit of her body.

After the show, the comedians gathered in the bar at the front of the venue where they accepted their accolades from the lingering audience. I watched Alex get a little mobbed by folks who seemed like long-time fans of hers. I sipped another drink and chatted with Dev as we leaned against the bar. After about half an hour, Alex finally made her way over.

I could feel my gaze shift as I looked at her, and I was certain she could see what I was thinking. She wrapped her arms around me and I kissed her on the cheek, returning her warm hug. I could see her being eyed desirously by several other people. And that did something to my heart. And my body.

"You were incredible up there," I whispered in her ear.

"Thank you," she whispered back. She pulled away and exchanged a kiss with Dev. As they stood chatting, all I could do was stand there, wanting. I could barely hear them through my desire.

Dev caught my eye. "It looks like you better get out of here," he told Alex, nodding his head toward me.

"Yeah?" She turned to me and I bit my bottom lip and nodded.

"She's looking at you like you're the first meal she's about to have in weeks. Go satisfy that look off her face."

Dev kissed Alex's temple and my cheek. "Seriously, please don't be this horny tomorrow. I won't be able to get through our scene."

I giggled and wrinkled my nose at him, slapping his ass as he walked past me and out the door.

Alex's deep brown eyes blazed into mine when I turned back.

"We're getting in a cab right now," she said.

"Yep." I slapped my drink down and we tried not to run out of the place.

§

The candlelight was soft and romantic. Neko Case serenaded us from the speaker in the corner of the room. Alex stepped toward me. "Paige, I don't want to push you. But if you're sure, I've never wanted anything more than this."

In response, I gently put my hands on either side of her face and brushed my lips with hers. I deepened the kiss, my tongue sliding over her teeth, and I began to unbutton her shirt.

"I promise you," I said between kisses, "This is all that's happening in the world right now. It's all I want to do."

She pulled back and met my gaze, that intense look that I had thought about every day since our first kiss seeming different in this moment. Something deeper was behind it, not just desire, but deep intention. "Okay," she said simply.

She took over, which made my heart pound and my whole body shiver. Her lips were on mine as she pulled off her pants. Then she stepped back and I watched as she stripped down to her underwear. I felt greedy with desire, wanting to touch every inch of her creamy skin bathed in the candlelight. My breathing deepened as I gazed at her from the bed.

She met my gaze and slowly stepped toward me. I sat back on my elbows and she straddled my lap. She brushed my long hair back off of my shoulders and I felt featherlight kisses along my collar bone. I sighed in pleasure. Her fingertips found the bottom of my shirt and I sat forward and raised my arms. She pulled the shirt off of me with a flourish and gasped aloud. We hadn't been this naked with each other yet and I shuddered under her. I wanted her hands, her mouth, her teeth, everywhere.

Taking deep breaths, she trailed her fingers down my neck to my breasts and I inhaled sharply, arching my back. She pulled back, her look questioning, fiery, wanting. I wanted so much more than her sweet caress. I put my hand on the small of her back and brushed my lips along her throat. She moaned.

I smiled wryly and leaned back on my elbows. She was above me, soft and beautiful and perfect. "I'm all yours," I said. "Do with me what you will."

Alex inhaled sharply, those words seeming to break something down. She smiled devilishly and stood. With a fervor I hadn't seen from her before, she pulled my skirt off and threw it over her shoulder. I laughed aloud as she slid herself on top of me. I could barely register the rush of her skin before her lips were on mine again, fierce and passionate. No longer hesitant.

"Paige," she moaned into my neck. She nipped and licked all the way down my body. She laced her fingers through my underwear and looked up at me again. I was on fire, burning beneath her.

"Alex, I want you. Please." I was begging, desperate to be closer to her. I could barely see for want of her. A smile snuck across her face and I watched her lick my hip bone. I groaned and fell back again. She snaked the panties down my legs and stood on her knees at the bottom of the bed. Triumphantly, she tossed them aside and I practically purred in anticipation. She kissed her way up my legs and my inner thighs started to quiver. And then...

Oh my.

Her tongue, her fingers... I was floating, falling as she swirled her tongue on my bundle of nerves. Her fingers curled inside of me and I raised my hips off the bed as I built toward my release, gasping for breath.

I could barely tell where she ended and I began. I bucked against her, wanting more, more, more, until I couldn't hold back any longer. I tangled my hands in her hair and cried out her name, shaking with the most intense orgasm I had ever had.

As I tried to remember my own name, she kissed her way up my body, grinning and clearly self-satisfied. I felt her tongue brush along my breast, my neck, my ear. She lay next to me, tracing a line from my hip to my throat with her fingertip. I was helpless. Spent. Electrified. New.

"You're the most magnificent woman I have ever seen," she whispered.

I looked up at her and traced her lips with my thumb. "You're not so bad yourself."

Softly, she leaned over and nibbled on my lip. I took her bottom lip between my teeth and caressed her waist, moving my hand up to cup her breast. I brushed my thumb over her nipple and she gasped. Confidently, I gently pushed her over and gazed into her eyes. As I slid down her body, I said, "Let me know if you have any instructions."

Twenty minutes later, our bodies were completely tangled together and I kissed Alex on her nose. "I cannot believe I haven't been doing that my entire adult sex life."

She chuckled. "Neither can I. You're a fast learner."

"It's not like I hadn't fantasized about it before. But that was better than I ever imagined."

She burrowed her face into my shoulder and we nuzzled for a few wonderful moments. I turned over onto my side and she did the same. We gazed into one another's eyes long enough to increase my breathing, to feel my chest flush with pleasure again. I caressed her smooth cheek and she closed her eyes with a smile.

This was no one time thing. This was no aching, dangerous, desperate affair. This was real, and I was falling for her hard. We fell asleep naked and tangled together, minds and hearts both.

§

"Is it weird how much I'm going to miss you? You've become a huge part of my weekends," Alex told me as we stood at the stairs leading to the El the next afternoon.

Without a car, I had to make quite a journey: the El down to Ogilvie Train Station in the Loop, hop on a Metra train for a couple of hours to the Harvard station in Wisconsin, and then be picked up by my dad for the half hour drive to Elkhorn: population around ten thousand, and too many of them my high school ex-boyfriends. It was a long day, but worth it.

I was looking forward to seeing him and my brothers and all of my nieces and nephews. I had missed their faces since seeing them at Christmas last year, and I was so glad to be closer than I had been in New York. That didn't mean I wasn't going to miss Alex though.

I burrowed my face into her neck. "I'll miss you too, but I'll be back for Sunday night lazies." This had become a favorite ritual of ours. We would order takeout and watch whatever was on HBO, and now we would get to slowly make love to gear up for the week. I couldn't seem to get enough of her. It was total bliss. I didn't know what the future would hold, especially if the show went well and I was asked to do the Broadway run. But for now, I was living in the moment, every one of them filled with her.

§

"Dad!" I stepped out of the station and into the parking lot where my dad leaned against his beat-up old Honda. He refused to replace it until it completely fell apart. He wore his usual uniform of t-shirt, old jeans, and construction boots, which he claimed were the only comfortable shoes in America. He'd worked construction his whole life and had retired to become an independent contractor, doing odd jobs around Elkhorn for folks who needed repairs or landscaping or plumbing.

Still fit at sixty, with a full head of salt and pepper hair, he strode toward me with purpose. He was a jack-of-all-trades, my dad, and we'd grown up learning how to do everything from him. That's how I knew how to change a tire and fix a running toilet without calling AAA or any landlord.

"Little One!" He caught me up in a fierce bear hug and I got a little overcome with emotions. I had missed him.

"Hi, Dad."

"Hey, kid. I missed you buckets."

"Missed you, too."

He took my weekender bag and put it in the trunk as I settled into the passenger seat. We spent the ride going back and forth over the basics: brothers, old friends, and how my work was going.

At a stoplight in the middle of Elkhorn's picturesque downtown, overflowing with May flowers, he turned to me. "I'm so proud of you, Little One. I'm just so proud."

He wasn't an effusive man, but he made sure to show us how much we were loved. I patted his arm. "Thanks, Dad."

We pulled up to our old Victorian house just outside of the town square and the front door flew open. I climbed out of the car and was bombarded by several little bodies scrambling to hug me all at once. I was buried in limbs and their sweet little voices.

"Auntie Paige, we missed you!"

"I'm so glad you're here!"

"I have dinosaurs, do you want to see them?"

"We have so much to show you, come on!"

A little hand tugged on mine, one of my nephews. Three little imps were dancing around me, desperate for my attention, and I was filled with so much love I nearly teared up again.

My brother Tom loped down the front porch steps with his youngest, Holly, in his arms. "August, Daniel, Margot, come on. Give your Aunt Paige some breathing room." He looked more like my dad than he ever had.

I let him squeeze me into a one-armed bear hug, as I smooched Holly on her chunky little cheek and smiled up at him. "Hey, brother."

"Hey, sister." He squeezed me once more before letting me go. I saw Josh and Sam over his shoulders. Josh, the oldest of us, was built like my dad and Tom, but Sam and I favored our mom. Smaller, finer-boned, dark wavy hair. Sam was only sixteen months older than me and we'd always been close. We all hugged and greeted each other, watched closely and affectionately by my dad from the front steps, where he held my bag.

I smiled up at him and I could swear there was a tear in his eye.

"All right, big city girl, let's get you inside and some food in you. Dad got a new smoker and the ribs are going to be excellent. I've been watching them all day." Josh slung his arm over my shoulders and we all made our way into the house.

It smelled of home. The smokiness from the back patio wafted in through the open windows, and I felt so much peace being with my family.

After an hour of letting my nieces and nephews lead me around the house, showing me everything I knew intimately since my dad never changed a thing, we all gathered around the farm table in the dining room off the kitchen. Josh proudly showed off his ribs on a huge platter. They looked delicious.

Tom's wife, Savannah, wrangled Daniel, while Tom strapped Holly into the booster chair. Their eldest, August, sat patiently in his new glasses, observing me. The chaos surrounding him rolled right off his back, but I could tell he was taking everything in. I'd told Tom on every visit that that kid was going to write great books.

Josh held Margot, his five-year-old, on his lap while he poured wine into all the glasses he could reach. His wife Angie was dishing out the corn, and everyone around me was chattering and happy. I caught Sam's eye across the table. He raised his glass at me with a grin. I tilted mine back.

My dad cleared his throat from the head of the table. We all settled down as he stood and smiled at all of us in turn. "It's a special day, today. Paige, we are so proud of you, and so glad you're so close to us now. I know it's not forever, but this family is everything to me, and I'm happy to see it back together. To Paige. Welcome home, Little One." He raised his glass and we all did the same, clinking ours together.

As we ate, I caught up on the lives of all the kids and my brothers and sisters-in-law. School was fun for August, a chore for Daniel, and Holly was growing too fast. Margot was going to skip kindergarten for first grade. Tom and Josh enjoyed working for Dad, and Angie's schedule at the hospital was grueling, but she loved being a nurse. Savannah was crushing it staying at home with the kids. Tom couldn't stop praising his wife for keeping their lives together. And Sam was still single, a graphic designer, and happy to live the bachelor life. He was the best uncle to all the kids. They loved him.

I was so happy to learn that my family were all content.

"So Paige," Josh said, after I'd eaten my fill of the delicious meal. Dad had taken the dishes into the kitchen with Angie and Savannah. The children had run off to the playroom and everything was a little less noisy. "Isn't this fun? Come back to us. The kids would love to have you around more often."

"What's that fancy city have that we don't?" Tom good-naturedly snickered at his own cliché. He drained his beer bottle. My dear brothers, fiercely protective as they were of me from outsiders, loved to needle me to the point where my head exploded.

"Literally everything." I rolled my eyes and stuck my tongue out at them.

"We've got theater here."

"Josh, Elkhorn Community Players, while it has its merits, isn't Broadway."

Tom chuckled. "You got that right. The last musical was atrocious."

"You still go?" I asked, a little surprised. Every dance competition, every talent show, every amateur musical, they were there to watch me shine and never made fun of me for it. Lots of other things, yes, but never that. I couldn't believe they still went to the little theater I'd grown up in.

"Absolutely. Season tickets." Josh grinned at me. This was the cutest thing I had ever heard. "But it's not seeing your sister on Broadway, that's for sure."

"There's nothing wrong with community theater." I was raised in it, and those memories were some of my fondest.

"There is when it's the junior version of *Rent* and instead of AIDS, it's diabetes."

My brother's laughter rang out raucously around the table and I joined them.

"But seriously, Paige. I know you're in this show now, but we miss you. Haven't you ever considered coming back?" Josh said.

I groaned and slumped back in my chair. I knew they were only half-serious. But still. "Guys, come on. I love this town. I loved growing up here. And I love seeing all of you. But it's not for me. I belong..." I gestured vaguely. Sam caught my eye and gave me a teasing grin. "Elkhorn will always be my hometown, but I have stuff to do. If this show goes well, I could have a lead on Broadway."

Sam's smile grew and he beamed at me. Tom and Josh let the teasing go and glowed with pride.

"That's right, she's a star," Sam said.

"Not yet." I propped my elbows on the table and put my chin in my hand, taking in the sight of three of the best men I knew. "I love you guys."

"Ahhh, we love you too." Josh leaned over and tousled my hair. I shoved his hand away while Tom got up and crooked his arm around my neck. He rubbed his fist into my head, and that's how our dad found us, as he had a thousand times over the years: seeing who could beat each other up first.

"Ice cream!" he called. He held out a tray with bowls of chocolate chunk and we heard galloping from upstairs. The children returned in full force, snatching up bowls and scarfing up the treat as fast as they could.

"You'll give yourself brain freeze," I told them. August looked up at me with a chocolatey grin.

"Worth it," he said, and dove in for more.

I joined him.

§

The flames in the fire pit in the backyard leapt high. The night sky twinkled above us with millions of stars. The kids had gone to their homes with Savannah and Angie, and my dad had feigned tiredness to allow the four of us to hang without censoring for a parent. Josh and Tom spoke more about all the kids' activities and personalities, the challenges of parenthood. Eventually, they drifted into talking about the Brewers season, which I tuned out a bit.

I always forgot about the stars on nights like this. My thoughts turned to Alex. She'd love it here. Everything was bright and clear and I could see her cuddling with me under a blanket on some distant autumn night. My brothers and their wives would sit around us, chatting like now, about nothing.

"Earth to Paige," Josh called across the flames.

I shook my head to clear my daydream. "Huh?"

"We were asking about the show. What's it like?"

I sat forward in my deck chair. "It's really fun, such a fantasy. I absolutely love my character. She goes from being someone who's pushed around to an absolute badass with a coterie of women warriors standing beside her. In fact--" I paused, deciding to test the waters with the news about

Cassandra's love interest. "--she falls in love with a woman at the end of the show."

The air around the fire stilled, if only for a moment.

"That's cool," Sam said.

"Yeah. Very cool," Tom echoed.

"So, you're a lesbian?" Josh asked bluntly.

I snorted.

He grinned at me sheepishly.

"It's not explicitly stated, just that Cassandra happens to fall in love with a woman."

"Like your pal, Dev," Josh said, pointing at me.

"Sure, a bit." They'd met Dev on one of their two trips to visit New York. Dev, who never once hid or was shy about who he was and what he wanted. He'd tried to shock my brothers, but they had pretty open minds.

"So the woman you fall in love with." Sam grinned at me from across the fire. "Is she hot?"

We dissolved into mirth. Could I have told them about Alex? Probably. It just didn't feel like the time. I knew they wouldn't judge, but maybe I just wanted to keep her to myself for now.

I changed the subject to Sam's little league game of 1997. We teased him about sitting in the grass while ignoring the ball, which got us reminiscing about every other little thing.

Two hours later, as we doused the fire and said our goodnights, I felt like my heart had grown three sizes. Josh pulled us all in to a four-way hug.

"I really missed you, dummies," I said.

They all squeezed a little tighter.

SEVEN

In the old Honda, I tried to keep my sadness at bay as I anticipated saying goodbye to my dad as we drove to the train station.

"Did your brothers give you a hard time about moving back last night?"

I chuckled. "Yeah, they did."

"For the record, I told them not to." His grin was lopsided when he snuck a look at me.

"Thanks, Dad."

"And as much as I hold on to hope that you'll someday be close by, I've always known you would take a different path."

"You did?"

He registered my surprise with a nod. "Absolutely. I knew from the day you were born. Of course, your mom was the one who told me so."

I looked up at the mention of my mom. He almost never talked about her. "Really?"

"She said to me, the first time I was holding you, 'We have to take care of this little one, Kevin. She's going to change the world.'" His voice caught a little at the end of his sentence and I could feel a lump rise in my throat.

"That's when I started calling you Little One. I knew right that second. You were going to do great things."

"You never told me that."

He reached over and tenderly laid his hand on the back of my neck. "I never needed to. You set out to live your life exactly how you wanted to, right from the jump. Hell, you danced before you walked. I knew that I had to put you in classes right away. That's what your mom would have done."

I turned my head and looked out the window, my eyes filling with tears. I sniffled.

"I just want you to be happy, however that happens." His voice was thick with emotion. I was touched.

"I'm really happy, Dad."

"Promise?"

"Promise."

He brought his hand back to the wheel and we drove a few miles in comfortable silence. I knew he was probably reminiscing about mom.

However that happens, he had said. I couldn't help but wonder if he somehow knew. Maybe he'd always known. I wasn't ready to say it out loud to him yet, but I could feel the weight of not telling him about Alex, about the truth, fill my heart.

We pulled into the station parking lot and got out. Dad removed my bag from the trunk, set it on the ground, and wrapped me in another bear hug. "It's nice to have you so close, Little One. You come back anytime."

"I will. I love you, Dad."

"Love you, too."

I picked up my bag and walked to the doors to the station, turning around for one more wave goodbye. He was leaning against his car door and waved back, a pensive smile on his face.

I knew my dad would always accept me.

And this weekend proved that they would all love Alex.

§

I trudged up the sidewalk to my building, my bag weighing heavily on my shoulder. Being at home constantly surrounded by everyone was incredibly draining and the train rides had been long. I needed a long, hot shower. I had a lot to think about.

"Hello, traveler."

I looked up, startled. Alex stood in front of my building holding a takeout bag and giving me a smile that made me feel like she knew all my secrets. My heart warmed at the sight of her, and all thoughts of my family fell away. I couldn't believe that someone was surprising me like this. "Is this a romantic comedy? Are you really here right now?"

"I don't know. Can you smell the pad Thai?" She held up the bag and I sniffed. Delicious.

"You're not just a daydream, then."

She cupped my face in her free hand and gave me a soft kiss on the lips. "Nope."

"I'm starving." Grinning, I led her into the building and my studio, where she set up the Thai food on the coffee table in front of the love seat. Gratefully, I heaved my bag onto my bed.

"Seems pretty heavy when you were only gone for the weekend," she observed.

"A girl needs her creature comforts," I said. The kit of skin care, hair care, and various other self-care items was pretty heavy when I pulled it out of the bag.

"Is that the stuff that makes you smell the way you do?"

I nodded. "I hope that's a good thing."

She stood up and strode over to me purposefully. Her nose touched mine and her hands found my waist. Our lips met and then she sniffed my neck and collarbone. I couldn't believe that these tiny gestures were setting such a fire in me. I longed for her, even though she was right in front of me.

"I noticed your hair smelled like strawberries the night we met. And your skin smells like peaches in the summertime." She brought my wrist up to her mouth and kissed it delicately, savoring me.

I sighed, relishing the close contact. "Well, not right now. I just traveled for about four hours and have niece and nephew handprints all over me. I'm going to take a quick shower."

She met my eyes and pouted adorably. "But... peaches..."

"Care to join me?" I slipped my hand around her waist.

In one fluid motion, she pulled her shirt over her head. "Nowhere I'd rather be."

Giggling, I started to strip as I followed her to the bathroom. Our food was cold when we finally got to it, but it was worth it.

§

"That was good, Paige, but can you pull it back just a little bit here? While it's a declaration of love, Cassandra doesn't want to scare Monet away from her."

I nodded, chewing my lip. "Will do." The stage manager, Melissa, called for a union break and I retreated to a corner of the studio.

It was Wednesday, the week after my trip home, and I was learning the new pages in which Cassandra fell in love. I couldn't help but think it was a little on the nose for my life, but I rolled with it anyway. Besides, I wasn't falling in love. Though Alex was someone fun and wonderful, I was trying--pretty unsuccessfully--not to get too attached.

Dev threw himself into a chair next to me, heaving a dramatic sigh. He noted the look on my face. "I think you're doing great," he said. He could obviously sense that I wasn't happy with my performance today. "You just got the pages. Give yourself a little time, okay?"

I turned to him, grateful for the vote of confidence. "Thanks, Dev."

"Can't help but see the parallels, here."

I snickered. "I know. I was just thinking it's a bit on the nose."

"How are things going with her?" He sipped from his water bottle, being very obvious about wanting some gossip.

I couldn't help the smile that stole across my face, even in my current state of anxiety. "She's pretty incredible. We just seem to fit. Everything is like a dream right now. My career, my love life. It's just..."

Dev looked over at me when I trailed off, a knowing look in his eyes. "I can see two complications."

"Do tell."

"One, you're not long for Chicago and she is, as previously discussed. Two, you saw your family this weekend, and that might have been disorienting for your newly-bi brain."

I tapped my finger to my nose three times. "They were pretty cool, actually. I didn't tell them about Alex, but I did tell them Cassandra falls in love with a woman. All they wanted to know is if she was hot." *Hot* came out of me like a frat bro at a party.

Dev snickered. "Well that's good to hear. You wouldn't always get that from small town Wisconsin."

I nodded. "I feel lucky. I know in my heart they'll accept me, accept Alex, but I am a little nervous about telling them. It's a big change. I don't want to spend one second wondering if they'll still love me."

"They'll still love you, Paige. But it will change. I'm not going to sugarcoat that. It did for me, and every other queer kid."

"Except Alex, whose parents practically came out for her." We both chuckled.

"There are the lucky few." Dev stood and stretched his arms over his head, making sure I got a peek at his toned abs.

I nodded appreciatively at his midsection. "Thanks for listening. And for the eye candy."

He grinned. "Always."

"All right, we're back! Can I get my ensemble out here for the Act Two, Scene Three?" Andrea called. Dev groaned. That was his most physical number.

"Hey, you got this, too."

He lightly punched me in the shoulder and then took his place in the center of the room.

§

The late-May sun glared hot over me the next Saturday as I made my way to Alex's apartment. Today was the day she'd promised a religious experience: a Cubs game at

Wrigley Field. She wouldn't hear that I had been there before, several times in my youth, to watch Brewers *v.* Cubs.

"Trust me, the experience with me, down on the third baseline, is going to be totally new for you," she'd proclaimed. A die-hard fan, she'd told me that the 2016 World Series win was one of the best nights of her life.

I could take or leave sports, especially baseball, which I'd always found a bit tedious. But when her eyes lit up as she talked about the line up or the night of that big win, I couldn't help but melt. I was ready for some beers and a hot dog and a quintessential Chicago summer experience.

"I am ready to be a changed woman," I declared, upon entering her apartment.

"I hope so, because that is absolutely what you'll be at the end of today." Alex emerged from her bedroom, Sammy at her heels. She was entirely decked out in gear: a bright blue Cubs hat, a jersey from the 2016 win under which she wore a Cubs tank top. Even her socks bore the cute bear logo.

I was an absolute puddle. What an adorable little dork.

"You can't wear that!" she exclaimed as she took in what I was wearing. I glanced down at the old Cubs *v.* Brewers t-shirt, which I'd knotted over my stomach, and jean shorts.

"Why not?"

"Because I cannot be seen with an out Brewers fan." She hissed the last three words. Her expression was so incredulous, I started to laugh.

"This is the only thing I have that has the Cubs on it at all."

"Well hopefully folks will just know that you got it at that game and not that you actually like the *Brewers*." She scrunched up her nose adorably.

I stepped closer to her and cupped her face gently in my hands. "I promise to be a convert by the end of the day. Besides, they're playing the Mets." My lips found hers and we sank into the kiss. She ran her hand along the bare patch of my stomach beneath the knot in the shirt.

"You better be."

"We cannot be a house divided," I said very seriously.

She broke out into a wide grin. "I can't wait to share this with you."

"Me, too."

I had never seen her so amped up. She trotted down the street to the Red Line station, jabbering all the way about today's lineup and the Cubs' chances. I could feel myself going all gooey inside. There is nothing as sweet as listening to someone be enthusiastic about something they love. Now I understood why she let me yammer on about the show on our first date. I could feel the gate I had put up over my heart giving even more. But I couldn't let myself fall for her. Not completely. We were going to have to break- up eventually.

But not today. Today was for joy.

Compared to everything we soon encountered at the Addison Red Line station, Alex looked completely normal. All I could see was a sea of blue and white as we hopped down the stairs and neared Wrigley Field. Everywhere I looked, people were decked out in Cubs hats, t-shirts, shorts, boas, wristbands, socks. I didn't remember this from the games of my youth.

People spilled out onto Clark Street from the bevy of bars and my ears were assailed with a chant of "Let's go, Cubbies!" in a staccato rhythm. The atmosphere was completely joyous, the possibility of winning hanging in the air. I gave myself over to the enthusiasm and let Alex guide me through the throng.

In front of the stadium, Alex bought a bag of peanuts in the shell and a Cubs hat. She turned to me, met my eyes, and stepped closer. As if lowering a crown, she placed the hat on my head. I smiled regally and gave her a Queen's wave.

That blazing look returned to her eyes. "Okay, that's really doing something for me."

"Oh yeah?" I stepped closer to her, trailing my fingers down her arm until I caught her hand. I was ready to knock her socks off. "I think David Ross is the best manager this team has ever had." My words came out in a purr and I knew this would have the effect that it did.

Alex stepped back from me, a hand over her heart. She pretended to gasp for air and fanned herself. "You just invoked the name of Grandpa Rossie. I am *beside* myself."

I shrugged and wiggled my eyebrows at her.

"Did you do *research*?"

I held my thumb and forefinger an inch apart. "Maybe a little."

She nearly flung herself at me and caught me up in a kiss. "Watch out, you. I'm going to fall for you in front of Harry Carey." She pointed to the statue behind her.

I chuckled a bit but was thrown by her words. Our relationship had an end date. I hoped she wasn't falling too hard.

Like I totally was.

Throwing that thought out of my brain, I took her hand and we got in line to go into the stadium. We crossed through the metal detectors and the concourse, the energy buzzing around us, and I followed Alex up a tunnel and out into the brilliant sunshine. She turned around as I gazed at the field.

"Welcome to the Friendly Confines," she said reverently, her arms thrown wide.

I took in the whole of Wrigley, having only ever experienced it from the bleachers. The third baseline was in front of us and Alex led us down to her family's season ticket seats. I turned on the spot, looking up into the stands, listening to the voices of the vendors calling out. Everyone I saw looked happy, the beer was already flowing, and I could feel the magic of this place.

I turned to Alex, whose expression was full of joy. "This is the most all-American and wholesome I have ever felt, I think."

"I'm so happy that you're here."

We settled into our seats and I bought us our first round of beers. As the game began, Alex cheered and booed and I was swept right along with her. We sang along with the organist's renditions of pop songs, and the players' individual walk-up songs, one of which was "This World Will Remember Me" from *Bonnie and Clyde*. There was a musical theater enthusiast on the team, and that made me smile. The Cubs were up at the seventh inning stretch and a local news anchor performed "Take Me Out to the Ballgame." I kept watching Alex watch the game. Her expression was intense and focused on each play, and I loved seeing her love something so much.

Then the Cubs were down by two at the bottom of the ninth and things were not looking good. There was one out left with players on second and third. Unfortunately, the next batter was not the Cubs best, so there was little hope. I was shocked at how the atmosphere changed. The people around us were grumbling, trying to decipher how the Cubs were going to pull this one out. Many were packing up their things and leaving, beers half-drunk and kids complaining.

But somehow they did it. The batter smashed the ball into the stands at right field, a home run. The Cubs took the game.

Absolute euphoria. The stands exploded with screaming and cheering and "Go, Cubs, Go" played over the loudspeakers. Alex was shrieking and jumping up and down. I jumped too but kept the yelling to a minimum. I could only imagine the look on Andrea's face if I blew out my voice because of a sports game.

Alex turned to me, her expression ecstatic, and she threw her arms around my neck and planted a kiss on my lips that could only be described as exultant. I smiled through her kiss and gave it right back.

As we turned to leave, I heard a gruff voice shout, "Hey!" A mustachioed man who had sat behind us was glaring right at me. I frowned at him, not intending to give him any satisfaction.

"Hey, are you serious with that?"

I looked around unsure if this man was talking to me. Was it the kiss, in this, one of the gayest cities in the world? I hoped not. Because I was ready to fight if that were the case. No homophobia on Alex's turf. Not today, sir.

"That Brewers shirt. What's the matter with you?" the man yelled at me. Then I caught his expression. His glare was replaced by a good-natured smile.

Alex was standing behind me and I knew she had no idea what had just gone through my head in that three second pause. I gave the man a shrug and a smirk. Alex, coming down from her euphoria, found this hilarious and razzed me about being a Brewers fan all the way back to her place.

While I laughed along with her, I thought about how ready I was to fight to defend her. And us.

EIGHT

After the game and gigantic slices of pizza, I promised my body a vegetable or two later so I wouldn't collapse in rehearsal. Then I lay with my head on Alex's shoulder and she absentmindedly caressed my back. I was in a state of complete bliss when she took me by surprise.

"Paige, I have to ask you something."

I raised my head and smiled dreamily at her. "Anything."

"I need to know where you see this going. If anywhere at all." Her expression had turned serious and she sat up, propping a pillow behind her back. I joined her against the headboard, unable to look at her while we had this conversation. A heavy silence settled between us and I took a deep breath.

"I thought we agreed to enjoy the time we have together." I wrapped my arms around my knees, avoiding her gaze.

"We did. We did. But..." She reached over and twirled my hair through her fingers. "I am starting to feel real things, and I wanted to ask where you were."

I turned my head and looked at her. She was gazing at my hair in her hand. I stroked my finger down her thigh as I said hesitantly, "To be honest, I'm not really sure. I don't actually live here. And I kind of promised myself I wouldn't date anyone while I'm in Chicago. You just fell into my lap, and I couldn't stop myself. I really, really like you. But I don't know how serious we can be." It broke my heart to say these words out loud, because despite my convictions, I was absolutely falling for Alex in every way and I didn't want it to end. But here she was, crashing reality into us after such a beautiful day. I curled around my knees again, feeling sulky. "It isn't going to end anytime soon. We have months."

"Right, but the thing is, I am really invested in you." Alex tugged her knees up to her chest and mirrored my pose. I looked over at her. She snuck a glance at my face and I wanted to kiss the freckles on her nose.

"Invested?" I wrinkled my brow.

She nodded. "That's a bit clinical, I guess. I really like you, too. I have been waiting... I've been waiting for someone just like you for so long. And I want to keep going. I just needed to know where your heart is."

"My heart is right here." I took one of her hands and brought it to my lips. I kissed her palm. She cupped that same hand on my chin.

"Do you want to keep going?"

"Of course," I said, alarmed. I didn't know it was *this* kind of conversation. "Even if we have to part someday, it just feels right to be with you right now."

Her lips curved into a soft smile. "We're on the same page there."

I pulled her to me and she nestled into the curve of my neck. A perfect fit.

"I was also wondering how you're feeling about being a little more public. You know, social media stuff. Your family."

I took another deep breath, ready to shoot this idea down. I wasn't sure I was ready for that yet. "I don't know..."

I felt her still in my arms. "I know not everyone gets a coming out party, but I deserve to be with someone, even if there's an end date, who wants to shout my name from the rooftops."

A thousand memories flooded through me. What she was asking was exactly what I had wanted from Ethan all those years ago. My chest burned at the thought of her feeling the way I had felt then. I squeezed her closer.

"I'll tell my family soon. And until then, I will shout your name from every rooftop in Chicago." I nudged her cheek with my nose and lowered my lips to her smile. She caressed the side of my face and I was a puddle of desire again.

She broke the kiss and I reluctantly let her. "So what exactly did we just decide?"

"I think that we're girlfriends? Until we can't be anymore, at least. I definitely don't want to be with anyone else."

"Girlfriends. I like that." She pressed her lips to mine again, then pulled back and furrowed her brow in mock seriousness. "But don't go falling for me."

"Wouldn't dream of it," I lied.

She gave me that smile that made my heart soar. Her mood was abruptly lighter when she sat up. "Good. Wanna do a puzzle?"

"I do."

She hopped out of bed, pulled on a pair of silky shorts and a tank, and tossed me my own. We traipsed to the living room and she pulled out a 500-piece puzzle while I poured us some wine. As we concentrated on getting the border done and she chattered about a new client she was assisting, I had a sudden flash of our future. I quickly pushed it aside, but I couldn't help but see a little dog curled up with Sammy, furniture we'd chosen together, in a cozy flat somewhere, doing puzzles well into our eighties.

Shit.

May turned to June, and Alex continued to be springtime in human form, all warmth and light and beauty. Chicago in the summer was idyllic. When I wasn't rehearsing, we strolled along the lake and bought popsicles from carts. We had dinner with my castmates or Alex's friends on patios. We cheered maniacally for one of her friends at a roller derby match, tried our hand at batting cages, and spent plenty of time goofing off in her apartment. She demanded that I teach her the choreography to some of the songs from *Cabaret*. It was impossible not to laugh at her adorable attempts to replicate my moves.

"I can't even touch my toes, but I want to *dance*, Paige!" she'd say as she flung herself around her living room. My cheeks hurt from smiling so hard.

I sat in the audience for more of Alex's sets. She continued to amaze me with her wit. The audiences were enthralled by her every word. She was certainly going places.

"Honestly," she said at the end of a new set, "there is nothing better than dating a musical theater actor. Like, a legit one. She sings to me, folks. Isn't that amazing? Well, not *to* me. But kind of *at* me? It's a little aggressive, to be honest. And it's always that one from *Chicago*. The six merry murderesses one. Do you know that one, sir? You know, 'He ran into my knife ten times.'" A huge laugh. Here, she would pause and come to a big realization. "Maybe this isn't the right relationship for me."

And then she would wink at me. And then I would want to run up onstage and tell everyone she was mine.

While her career was flourishing in clubs all over Chicago, I was continuing to have trouble with the scene where Cassandra falls in love. I was playing too big, then too small, then again not enough and then again too much. I couldn't find the truth in it and I was unsure what to do. I was hoping they wouldn't cut the storyline just because I couldn't act.

"Stop doing this to yourself," Dev told me one night as I stomped out of the rehearsal building. I had barely said good night to the rest of the cast. I wheeled to face him.

"Doing what?" I was full of frustration, my hands balled into fists.

"Beating yourself up over that scene. Everything else you're doing is perfect."

I almost hissed at him. "So the scene *is* garbage. Thanks."

He rolled his eyes. "Only you would twist my words around like that."

"I'm not feeling very charitable at the moment." I crossed my arms over my chest.

"I think it's not even your fault. I have a feeling it's the way they've written it."

The glare I hit him with could have melted a mountain. "Don't try to do that, don't throw Toby under the bus just because I'm fucking it up."

Dev didn't get mad at me like I wanted him to. I wanted a fight and he just looked at me with pity.

"Wipe that look of your face." I stepped menacingly toward him.

"Why do you want to fight with me?" He crossed his arms in front of his chest, not giving an inch.

I shrugged. "Haven't had a good one in a while."

He sighed dramatically and rolled his eyes. "Say goodnight, Paige."

I bared my teeth at him. "Next time, fight me."

"Go drink a glass of wine. Or eat an edible. You've *got* this. You will get there. I promise."

"Stop being reasonable. It's infuriating." I glowered as I backed away.

"Love you."

"Love you, just not today." I stomped my way toward the El, hoping none of my other castmates were nearby. I knew what my frustration was. I couldn't find the truth of the scene. And that made me angry. And anger turned to irrationality. Which made me dramatic. And then I turned on Dev, who had no right to be so understanding. I calmed down as the train made its way north. I pulled out my phone and texted him.

Okay fine. I love you today, too.

He texted back immediately.

Thought so. Xoxoxo

I smiled to myself, then I cancelled my plans with Alex and went home to work on the scene. She was understanding, too. I was starting to think maybe I was the irrational one. Either way, I vowed to be better in rehearsal the next day.

But I wasn't. It wasn't working. I could tell my scene partner, Steph, who had brought Alex into my life, was also frustrated. She offered to work with me. But that didn't help because it wasn't about her. We had plenty of chemistry and she was great in the scene.

It was me. I was the one completely lost.

While Andrea was encouraging, I was completely beating myself up over this. I could feel that part of my brain, the part that I didn't let out most of the time, leak into my consciousness. It whispered how terrible I was, how I was never going to make it.

I was holding my head in my hands on my love seat rolling everything over in my head: the scene I couldn't get, the press I was going to have to start doing, my dad, my brothers, Alex. I could feel my anxiety build and build until it felt like I was going to explode.

There was a soft knock on my apartment door.

I had given Alex the front door code. I was sure it was her, and relief washed over me at the sight of her perfect face. She held up a brown paper bag.

"I come bearing sushi. You seem like you're not eating enough."

We'd hung out and gone on dates, but she could tell something was going on with the show, especially when I cancelled on her twice at the last minute. That was the good part about dating a fellow performer--we knew when to take things personally and when not to.

I stared at her for a few long moments, my breathing growing heavier.

She raised an eyebrow and the bag and jostled it up and down. "Sushi. Paige? Hello?"

I took the bag from her and pulled her inside. Eagerly, I set the sushi on the coffee table, pulled her bag off her shoulder, cupped her face in my hands, and kissed her fiercely, hoping I was conveying just what a lifesaver she was.

She returned my kiss with fervor. "If a salmon roll is going to get that reaction every time, I'm going to bring you sushi more often," she said when we came up for air.

I grinned sheepishly. "It's been a rough couple of weeks."

"I know. I could tell. I thought some protein might help."

I smooshed my face into her neck. "You're the best," I practically groaned.

"I am an excellent girlfriend, if I do say so myself." She extracted herself from me and went to open the bag. As she began laying out the containers of sushi, I brought plates and napkins over. We opened the chopsticks and I popped a piece of dragon roll into my mouth. I moaned a little. "Mmm, you were absolutely right. I needed sustenance."

"I win best girlfriend," Alex said as she took in my pleasure, satisfaction lighting up her eyes.

"It's not a competition."

"True. But I win, though." She grinned at me and tossed an edamame bean in the air, catching it expertly in her mouth.

She definitely won.

"Do you want to talk about it?" she asked me as we polished off the last of the spicy tuna roll.

"About what?" I leaned back into the loveseat and patted my stomach. "I am sated."

"The show. What's going on? You were so confident about it in the beginning. What changed?"

I sighed, a bit of the anxiety returning. I looked into Alex's open face and knew she would understand this. "It's the declaration of love scene. I can't find the truth of it. This show is a bit of a spectacle, but this scene is tender and sweet. Smaller. And for some reason, everything I'm trying isn't working."

Alex crunched the sushi detritus into the recycling bin as she listened. With a pensive look on her face, she turned and stared at me for a few moments.

"Where's your script? Show me the scene."

I brought her my binder and flipped to the correct page. I could feel the familiar electricity begin to crackle in the space between us. She read the few pages over and I stood silently, waiting to see what she would do next.

"Would you like a little help from me?"

I felt the anxiety in my chest loosen its grip a fraction. "I would love that."

"It's been a while since I've done any real acting, so take whatever I say with a grain of salt. But I hate seeing you so tied up in knots, so I'll help however I can."

I sighed happily and kissed her softly. She gave me a grin and began pacing the room as she flipped through the pages.

"Okay," she finally said. "What we have here is a quiet scene that is-- I mean, it is extremely intimate. Is that what they're going for?"

I nodded.

She put a hand over her mouth, thoughtful, and I couldn't help smiling. I loved this take-charge side of her.

"I would guess it's difficult to do a love scene with no one," she concluded.

I chuckled. "Running it with Steph won't help. I'm the problem."

"You're a perfectionist."

"To a fault, generally."

She studied me again and I felt naked under her gaze. I had never seen this side of her before, and it was only intensifying what I was already feeling.

"So you're stuck. Why don't we run the scene and go from there."

"Okay."

Alex read from the script. I closed my eyes, conjuring Cassandra. I was already off-book, lines memorized, because I had done this what felt like a thousand times.

I performed the blocking effusively, my tiny apartment a far cry from the huge stage we would be on. I went through the lines. She responded.

It felt utterly, completely wrong.

After we finished, I turned to her, feeling absolutely hopeless. But then I looked in her eyes and the tingle of electricity flickered between us again. Her gaze was fierce, a look I knew well. Suddenly, she tossed the binder on the bed. With the exception of my bedside lamp, she turned off all the lights in the apartment. The lamp's red shade gave off an amber glow, making the small space suddenly romantic. Tunnel-of-love-proposal-scene-movie-montage romantic. My breath slowed.

After retrieving the binder, Alex turned to me again. "When have you felt the most in love?" Her husky voice was soft, quieter.

My heart began to pound as I considered her question. "I'm not sure what you mean."

"Well, for me," her tone was still soft, "it's in the dark. In those quiet moments, just before dawn. When an arm holds onto you and nothing else matters but the person sleeping next to you, their breathing steady. Grounding you. It's soft. Peaceful. Quiet. That's when I've felt love most profoundly."

I stilled. I could only gape at her.

She nailed it.

"That's it," I whispered. I closed my eyes and she gave me those few moments to collect my memories.

"Start again." Her command was gentle and I was ready.

This time, I contained myself, pulling from those pre-dawn half-dreamy moments in my life. And something wonderful happened. I could feel Cassandra falling, I could feel everything she had ever wanted guiding me along to finally declare her love for Steph's character, Monet. And it wasn't in that effusive, musical theater, big way. It was intimate and acute and true.

At the end of the scene when Cassandra and Monet kiss, we came together, and Alex tossed the binder onto the love seat. I looked deeply into her beautiful brown eyes and felt something pulling at my heart, a thread of gold from her to me that was only getting stronger. Something neither of us were looking forward to breaking.

She snaked her arms around my neck and gave me that fiery look. Feeling almost desperate, I crushed my lips to hers and moaned as she nipped my bottom lip. Her cherry lip gloss tasted delicious and I grasped the nape of her neck, the curve of her waist. Her hands tangled in my hair and I found the bare skin of her back as the kiss deepened. She pulled back a bit and ran her lips softly over mine, leaving them warm and wanting. Her gaze settled on mine.

I could tell she was thinking what I was. That even if we were acting, the love we had just declared was real and deep. She was breathing heavily and we gazed into each other's eyes for a few long, lingering moments.

"So... Just don't forget the quiet. When you feel love most profoundly." Her expression was searching, almost bemused.

I was rendered mute, holding her around the waist and falling into the deep infinity pools of her eyes. All of our protestations about getting into something serious ran through my head, and I knew they were gone now.

Oh boy.

NINE

The night that Alex helped me through that scene was the night both of our lives changed forever, though it went unsaid. There was no turning back, and no pretending anymore. We were in it. Deep.

And it was the best time of my life.

"I haven't heard from you in ages," Kat teased me over the phone after a rehearsal. June was passing by quickly, and I had been so caught up in the show and Alex that I had neglected my former roommate.

"I'm a dick, I'm sorry," I told her, remorse in my voice.

"GIFs of the Real Housewives do not a friendship make." She was scolding me now.

"I know, I know. I text other things."

"That's not real conversation."

I rolled my eyes, grinning. Kat was such an old soul sometimes. "Sorry, Mom."

"You better be. Download, please. Everything."

She used to say this to me after a long day. The kettle would whistle and we would sip our tea and "download" each other on whatever we'd missed in each other's days. I felt my throat get a little tight. I missed her.

"And start with the girlfriend."

I laughed out loud and told her about Alex. At length. She listened with her trademark patience as I gushed about the woman who had changed my life.

"So do you love her?" she said when I finished.

"I haven't said it out loud. We're both being shy about it because... well, you know, this has to end."

"Couldn't she make the comedy scene in New York work for her?"

A breath whooshed out of me. "I'm sure she could, but she has her classes and family here, and that is a whole other conversation."

The line went quiet. Kat was gearing up to say something real, I could feel it. "You sound so grounded about her. Usually you're much more dramatic about dating someone. But it sounds really steady. I love it."

I closed my eyes, letting memories of my past with men who wouldn't be available to me seep in. I had hated that feeling, and Alex was different, in literally every conceivable way. "I had no idea relationships could be like this. I don't question anything. She's so supportive and just really gets me. I feel seen with her."

"I'm so glad you figured it out and found her." Kat's voice was soft and she sounded genuinely pleased.

"Thanks, girl."

"I love you, girl. Now let me tell you about the newest dancer in my company. The *thighs* on him. You would die."

Kat chattered on about the new dancer and gave me the download on her life. I lay back on my bed, feeling the comfort of home in her voice. When we said goodbye, it was with a heavy heart and lots of promises to call and talk to each other more often.

My departure from Chicago was going to be difficult, but I was grateful I would have Kat to lean on when it happened.

§

"Baby's first pride!" Alex exclaimed when I walked into her apartment on the morning of the last Sunday of June. It also happened to be my thirtieth birthday. Sammy curled around my legs wearing a rainbow ribbon. Alex was wearing a short-sleeved button-down shirt and tiny, shiny green shorts, knee socks with the rainbow flag all over them, and her hair was full of glitter. On her wrists were rainbow cuffs and she wore a floral lei with pride colors around her neck.

She looked like magic.

"I can't wait. I'm so glad I decided to spend it with you. It's not my first, though. I was in the New York parade last year."

Like Broadway shows in New York, Broadway in Chicago always had a float in the city's Pride Parade. But this year I had declined the invitation to dance with my castmates and the casts of the other shows running next season. While they threw beads from our float, I would stake out a spot on the parade route with my girlfriend. We were going to celebrate my birthday in the gayest way possible.

"I got you a birthday present." Alex smiled secretly and handed me a rainbow patterned bag.

"I love presents!"

Her laughter rang out through her apartment. "You're supposed to say 'oh, you shouldn't have.'"

"Not my style, babe." I kissed her full on the mouth and then tore into my gift. Inside, I found a tank top that said *She is mine* on it, matching cuffs and lei, and tiny blue booty shorts. I squealed in excitement and looked up. Alex had taken the button down off revealing a matching tank that said *I am hers* on it.

I melted again. She was always doing that to me. Right there in her living room, I began stripping off my clothes to put on my new outfit.

"I really like that dancers just get naked wherever," Alex said as she watched.

"Oh, well, let me slow it down then." I began a ridiculous over-the-top burlesque dance, teasing her with glimpses of skin until I was just in my panties in front of her and we were both laughing so hard we were crying. I put on my new tank and pulled the booty shorts on as we calmed down.

"That was hilarious, but sometime I'm going to want you to give me a real striptease." Alex pulled my hips to hers and our lips crashed together. "Happy birthday."

"Thank you. For all of this."

Her gaze met mine and her expression softened. "Wouldn't trade it for the world." We kissed again, slower this time, building in intensity as her hands traveled under my new top. I moaned as her tongue trailed along my neck and felt her nibble at my earlobe. I opened my eyes for a brief second and noticed the time on her wall clock.

"We better go or we're going to get a bad spot," I told her reluctantly, my body still tingling as she pulled away.

She beamed at me. "I will birthday-worship you later. Let's go."

Alex had packed a small backpack with a flask of vodka, waters, and sunscreen which we applied liberally before we left. She lived near the middle of the parade route, so it would be an hour or so after it began that we would see anything, but we wanted to get a good spot on the curb.

The neighborhood was bursting with joy. We joined a throng of people of all shapes, sizes, gender expressions, and states of dress and walked to Halsted Street.

I have always loved Pride, but I came to it with a new appreciation this year. As we approached Halsted, the bass thump of dance music greeted us. It was an entire party in the street. Though it was not even eleven in the morning, Alex handed me the flask and I took a generous gulp. This was a day of revelry and debauchery and yes, pride, and I intended to celebrate it to its fullest. We had even been given the next day off because everyone on the production staff knew we'd all be useless and hoarse. And so would they, frankly.

We staked out a spot along the barriers on Halsted, miraculously under the shade of a tree. Speakers propped up in windows nearby were blasting Lady Gaga, Ariana Grande, and even a remix of "Candy Store" from *Heathers the Musical*. Around us, folks began to gather. The cacophony of *hellos* and *oh my god I haven't seen you in forever*s, the scream singing along to the music, the *who is she*s and the *where did they go*s grew louder and louder. Alex made friends with the women next to us and the couple next to me complimented me on my short shorts. A very buff man in angel wings and teensy briefs walked by handing out purple flowers to everyone. A young family with a stroller and a toddler staked out a spot down the block and the child waved a tiny Pride flag to everyone walking by.

Everyone, no matter who they were, was accepted here on the street in front of Scarlet Bar. I was taking it all in, the day getting a glow around the edges like it was already a memory I would cherish for years to come. I looked over at

Alex, who was animatedly chatting with the people next to her and felt a rush of affection so deep that I interrupted their conversation to press my lips to hers in gratitude.

Surprised, she pulled back and looked into my eyes.

"Thank you for helping me find out who I am," I told her.

Her expression melted into joy and she kissed me again. "Happy birthday, Paige."

"It's my birthday!" I shouted joyously. I was met with cheers and folks raised red Solo cups in my direction, wishing me a happy one.

Soon, after several more pulls on the flask for each of us, the first banner of the parade appeared. We cheered and waved at every float that went by, catching freebies and candy, beads, and stickers. I soon had a collection of rainbow beads around my neck and Alex pasted several stickers down both of our arms.

Drag queens in impossibly high heels walked and waved and danced, the Cubs and White Sox floats tossed out t-shirts, Chicago's aldermen and -women marched behind their banners, the first trans woman to anchor at a Chicago news station waved proudly from a convertible, high school and college bands played Diana Ross songs, drumlines and dancers performed. It was sensory overload, the vodka was coursing through my veins, and all I felt was complete and total joy.

When the Chicago Gay Men's Chorus stopped and sang "Make Them Hear You" from *Ragtime* a cappella, tears slid down my face, while Alex gripped my hand tightly. I turned to her and noticed a glistening in her eyes as well. She put her arm around my waist and we held each other close.

When the Broadway in Chicago float came by, Dev, who was dressed only in shorts like ours, ran over and kissed us both on the lips, which we welcomed. The rest of the cast waved and cheered from the float and I shouted, "I love you!" They were magnificent.

I was so grateful to be exactly where I was: next to Alex, surrounded by people living their truth out loud, in a city that celebrated Pride so big, it basically shut down the entire north side of Chicago.

The morning passed in a hazy, delicious rainbow of love and acceptance. Alex and I tripped along with the couple next to us, who had invited us to a house party after the parade was over.

"Y'all are such a cute couple. When's the wedding?" the one named Steve or possibly Jared asked. Alex and I looked into each other's faces and began to laugh uncontrollably, ignoring the question and the fact that this relationship was destined to end. We drank more from the flask and realized that was the end of our vodka.

Alex pouted and turned to the boys. She upended the flask and a sad drop of vodka splashed onto the sidewalk. "This party isn't BYOB is it?"

"Of course not, come on!" Darius or possibly Harold or maybe also James draped his arm around her shoulders and pulled her up the block. I would never properly learn their names, but I loved them for bringing us along.

We entered a side gate to a backyard where a keg was flowing and everyone cheered at our arrival. A karaoke machine was set up on the porch and drinks were shoved in our hands. The bass was thumping again, vintage Britney, and Alex and I floated from group to group. She was recognized by a few people and I loved watching her make everyone she met feel welcome and comfortable immediately. When she told a group of guys that I was in what would hopefully be a successful Broadway show, I was pulled in every direction. Selfies were demanded, and then I was shoved toward the karaoke machine and made to sing "Don't Rain on My Parade" three times in a row.

Alex cheered me on from the front of the crush of people, and then we found ourselves swept into the unfinished basement where colorful laser lights beamed and more music thumped, in the middle of a foam party. Someone had set up a machine that spit out bubbles and suds of foam and we were soon soaking wet and dancing in what felt like a dream. She put her arms around me and as bubbles were tossed and floating around us, her lips met mine. I thought maybe I had reached total nirvana with this woman in my arms, her soft lips searching mine, and then she whispered "Let's get out of here" and we were falling back up the stairs and walking back to her building, dancing down the sidewalk and giggling to beat the band.

Back inside Alex's building, our laughter faded as we walked up the stairs. We were sweaty and sticky and I felt like I'd just run a marathon. Alex took my hand and led me to her bedroom where she lit a few candles. She went into the bathroom and turned on the shower, then came back and lifted one of the strands of beads around my neck with her pinky.

"So. Good birthday?" She looked into my eyes and I fell again into the warmth of hers.

"Best birthday." I pulled a few strands of beads off, the limp, sad lei coming with them. She took off the rest, then her own, tossing them carelessly on the floor.

"I forgot to get you cake."

"I don't really like cake."

Steam began to flow out of the bathroom and we eagerly stripped our clothes off and stepped into the shower together. Her body was slick against mine as we washed off the glitter and peeled off the stickers. I chuckled at the spot where the beads had bled onto her sweaty neck, creating a rainbow tattoo of sorts, and wiped it away for her. Underneath the water, she ran her hands up my side and pulled me close. I tasted her mouth, vodka and gum, and stroked my tongue over hers.

That seemed to create something urgent in her, because she hastily reached over and turned off the shower, then dragged me, still dripping wet, to her bed. She laid me down and then she was on top of me, her body soft and warm from the shower. Her breath tickled my wet skin as she placed silky kisses all the way down my body. She stroked my inner thighs lightly and I fell open to her, giving myself to her completely. Slowly, methodically, she teased my skin with her tongue until I was begging for more of her.

When her fingers entered me, she curled them upwards, making me gasp. Her tongue swirled and pressed more urgently. I moaned with desire and was lost in bliss for what felt like hours. Pleasure was gathering inside of me, building to an explosion as she worked her magic. When I felt I almost couldn't take it anymore, she increased the pressure of her tongue and I burst, like a supernova, quaking against her as she slid up my body and lay beside me. I almost started laughing at the intensity, but instead turned my face to hers and kissed her slowly.

I stroked my hand down her breast, the dip of her waist, until I felt her wetness. She moaned and gasped against me as I searched her silkiness, but when I moved to go down on her, she stopped me.

"No," she rasped. "Look at me." She pushed her lips onto mine, then pulled back and gazed at me intently. She stroked her hand between my legs again and I groaned.

We melted together, our legs intertwining, hands and fingers stroking and probing, never tearing our eyes away from one another. I had never made love like this before. I had never felt so close, so trusted, so beloved by someone before. She shuddered against me, crying my name, and I followed seconds later.

Satiated, breathing hard, we curled into each other. She tenderly caressed my cheek and I felt a blossoming in my chest, that golden thread connecting our hearts shimmering, turning solid.

"Dammit," I whispered, knotting my eyebrows together as I looked into her perfect face.

She gave a little laugh, seeming to know what I was cursing. "Are you thinking what I'm thinking?"

I nodded. "It's happened." I took her hand still on my cheek and interlaced my fingers with hers. I brought it to my lips, closed my eyes, and kissed each one of her fingers.

She began to laugh and I joined in. She rolled over onto her stomach and buried her face in her pillow. "Oh no," she moaned.

"Oh no," I echoed. I stroked one finger down her spine and she visibly shivered under my touch. She turned to face me again.

I reached out and stroked her cheek. Her brown eyes twinkled in the moonlight, and I threw everything I thought about everything to the wind. Our laughter faded, our gazes locked, and I couldn't stop myself. This woman was everything. The words came out of me with no hesitation, no insecurity that she wouldn't say them back.

"I love you, Alex."

She gasped lightly, her eyes brightening. "I love you, Paige." She reached for me and I moved closer to her, wrapping my legs around hers.

Gazing deeply into my eyes, she said, "I think I loved you in that gross little bar. I think I loved you when you kissed me on the street. I think I loved you that whole month before we slept together, and I know, completely and totally know, that I love you now."

My heart hammered. I was rendered speechless. And while our future was completely uncertain, no one had ever seemed so sure of their love for me. "Ditto," I said. It was all I could manage as that golden thread strengthened.

She put her arms around me and brushed her lips over my eyelids, my cheek, my nose, until she finally brushed my lips. I pulled her closer, deepening the kiss, willing her to feel how much I loved her with every breath I took. I pulled away and the thought of leaving Chicago when the show was over flashed through my mind.

She seemed to understand exactly what I was thinking because she nodded and caressed my cheek, a tender, slightly apprehensive look in her eyes.

"We're in trouble, aren't we?"

TEN

Alex and I were totally, completely in love. But as that golden thread between us strengthened, 16both of our careers ramped up and we couldn't spend as much time together. Alex kept going up at comedy clubs, spending a lot of time working on new material. And my show was solidifying into what it would become. I was learning new choreography, memorizing new pages, and beginning to feel the responsibility of leading my company on this journey. As July went on, we were thinking about the big Broadway in Chicago concert in Millennium Park. We were leaning heavily on the big numbers in rehearsal, presuming that's what we would be performing. I was nervous, but I was ready.

And we finally had a title: *On Her Own*. It had gone through several iterations and finally landed there. I liked it. Now that it was named, the show had an Instagram and began to post rehearsal teases to the rabid Broadway fanbase. And my personal follower count exploded.

It was suddenly all very real.

Lying in bed one Sunday morning, Alex burrowed into her pillow next to me and glanced at my phone as I scrolled.

She huffed. "I cannot believe you got more followers than me in a week. One week!"

"I cannot believe you still can't comprehend how nuts the Broadway fanbase is. I love them. It's incredible."

"What do you think about taking our relationship to social media?"

"Whoa whoa whoa. Are you trying to put a ring on it?" I teased. She chuckled and kissed my shoulder. I thought about it for a moment. "Going public on the socials. I'm into it. But I have to talk to my family first. I don't think they'd like finding out I'm bi from an insta post."

"What about the rest of your pals?"

I rolled my eyes and turned to look at her. "Honestly? Most of them know about you. And the ones that don't won't care. Or be surprised."

A dreamy smile made its way across Alex's face. She slithered closer me, her silky skin against mine, and she nibbled my neck. "Have you been talking about me?" she purred.

I tossed my phone aside and wrapped my arms around her. "How could I not?" My lips met hers, pillowy soft. She moved on top of me and deepened her touch.

We were late to brunch with Dev, who was so pleased with the satisfied looks on our faces that he didn't even make us apologize.

§

"Call me if you need me." Alex held my hands tightly in front of the El. I was once again Wisconsin-bound, and I was jangling with nerves. I was certain my family would be understanding, but that didn't mean I wasn't about to drop a personal-life-news-bomb on them.

The July sun was beating down and the humidity that was so unique to the Midwest was soaking my skin. I couldn't tell if it was nerves or the weather that was making me so sweaty. "I will, I promise. I'm sure it's going to be fine."

She gently took my face in her hands. "I love you." She kissed my nose, then my lips. I felt so cherished by her, so incredibly grounded and loved. I hugged her close.

"Love you, too. Call you after I tell them."

"Travel safe." I held her hand for one more moment and we gazed at each other. I could see a sadness in the deep pools of her brown eyes as I let go and walked up the steps to the train. It was nice to know I would be missed.

Once downtown, I boarded the Metra train, stowed my bag under the seat, and took out a notebook and pen. I curled up and watched the city fade in the distance as the train made its way out of Chicago and north toward Wisconsin. I twirled the pen between my fingers, thinking about Alex. I began to write down everything I loved about her.

1. Her laugh, her smile
2. Her dry sense of humor, and the way she gets mine
3. The spark I feel every time she touches me, the mind-blowing orgasms

4. How supportive she is, and how she seems to know when I need more or less
5. The way she grew up, her open mind, her open heart
6. Her passion for romantic comedies, which I'm actually not allowed to repeat to anyone

The list kept getting longer. Pages. I guess I was trying to figure out what on earth was going to happen with us. Because I loved her deeply, in a way I had never felt about anyone. With Alex, I didn't question anything. She was solid and steady, and our love was true. It was the first time I had ever felt this way, and I could see us together for a long time. But the logistics of our lives were in the way. Could we somehow make it work? I wasn't sure, but I definitely didn't want it to end. My mind reeled with the possibilities.

Perhaps I could live without the planning. I thought of what my schedule would soon be like: eight shows a week, only one day a week free. How were we going to keep up this movie montage we'd been in for these past few months?

I tossed down my pen and closed the notebook. I nestled my face into my palm and stared out the window. However hard it would be, I decided I would let the future unfold how it may. At least I got this time with her. I didn't want to think about goodbye.

My dad was outside the station again, in the same outfit, with the same Honda, and the same bear hug. He asked me about the show on the way to our house and I nattered on about castmates and scenes and songs. He was genuinely interested. He always was.

I was once again attacked by little ones at the house and they pulled me around for a good hour before we all sat down to dinner. I looked around at my brothers and their partners, my dad at the head of the table joking with my nephew. I felt such love for them I feared I might explode. The chatter was noisy and fun, the love was palpable. My hands were a little shaky, but I knew I didn't have anything to be nervous about. These were my people, the ones who had known me intimately since birth. They'd wiped my tears, bandaged banged up knees, bought me every dance shoe and tutu, tolerated my voice lessons, and were front row to every performance I had ever been in.

They loved me to pieces.

I had nothing to fear.

I cleared my throat and clinked my butter knife against my wine glass.

All eyes were on me, and Holly started banging her plastic fork on her high-chair tray. I laughed at her and reached over to pinch her chubby cheek before saying, "I have something to tell you all."

Sam sat forward in his chair, elbows on the table and palms steepled in front of his face. Josh stole a look at Tom and they shared a secret grin, like they had discussed something like this happening and knew where it was going.

Doubt it.

I lowered gaze to the table, bit my lip, and took a deep breath. I looked at the faces I'd known all my life in turn.

"I'm in love," I said simply. I let it sink in.

Josh whooped with joy and pulled Angie to him. He gave her a kiss full on the lips, prompting an *ewww* from August.

Tom exclaimed, "I knew it!"

My dad tipped his glass at me and said, "I'm glad to hear that, honey."

Savannah and Angie began to trip over themselves with questions in turn. "Who is he? What's his name? Where is he from? Are you going to stay in Chicago permanently?"

Only Sam had remained quiet. I could feel his eyes on me. So close everyone thought we were twins growing up, I knew he sensed that wasn't the end. I met his gaze.

"Her name is Alex," I said loudly over the din.

Time froze for just one second. It was the longest second I had ever lived through and I wanted to sink through the floor and escape. Until my dad spoke.

"Well that's great, Little One, what does she do?"

Relieved, I stammered out that Alex was a comedian with a day job and was then peppered with questions by all of them: how did we meet, what was she like, when was she coming to visit...

Once answered, I told the table in general, "Thank you for not being weird."

Josh rolled his eyes at me. "We're just happy you're happy, kid. I bet Alex is great. Is she really that funny?"

"The real question is," said Sam, a twinkle in his eye, "is she hot?"

I snorted and gave him the finger.

"Oooh! That's naughty!" August cried. But we were all laughing.

As we traipsed to the kitchen to clean up and argue over who was going to do the dishes, who would empty the dishwasher, and what leftovers my brothers would get to take, it struck me that I had never felt so loved in all my life.

I couldn't wait for them to meet Alex.

§

"I'm so glad they took it well. But I'm up in ten minutes, I have to go."

Alex was doing an open mic, so I was happy I'd caught her before she went on. I didn't want her to be anxious. "No problem. I'll talk to you later. Have a good set. I love you." It still made me blush.

I could hear the smile in her voice. "Love you, too."

I ended the call and set the phone at my side. I turned at the creak of the floorboards behind me.

"Good view, huh?"

Josh, Tom, and their families had gone home a while ago, and my dad went upstairs to bed. Sam stood behind me, backlit by the light of the kitchen, holding two beers. I smiled at him from my spot on the steps of the patio leading out into the yard and patted the wood next to me.

He ambled over in that slow and steady way of his, handed me a beer, and moaned as he sat down. "My body is getting old."

I nudged his shoulder with my own. "You're only thirty-one, Sam. You can't possibly feel that old."

He grinned at the sky and let the peace settle between us. The fireflies blinked in the yard and I felt as if all the summer nights we'd spent out here were flashing by. There we were with a tiny tent and flashlights, "camping." A little Sam was pushing a little Paige on the old swing set that had since been torn down. Sam at eleven, teaching me to kick a soccer ball and me failing. Me at twelve, teaching him to do an arabesque and him failing spectacularly. Teenaged us, sneaking a wine cooler and giggling, hidden in the shadows of the tree line at the edge of the property. Bundled up in blankets and hoodies, hanging out with our first boyfriend and girlfriend.

The specters of a life lived almost inseparably were floating all over the backyard. I sighed contentedly. Sam was a part of me.

He seemed to sense I was feeling nostalgic and gazed up at the stars. "I know cities have their merits, but it really doesn't get any better than this."

"We had a good childhood, didn't we?"

"Only place I'd want to grow up." He paused and snuck a glance over at me. He took a drag on his beer bottle. "But I understand why you would want to leave. You were always built for bigger things than this. I've always admired that about you. You made your own way. And look at you now."

"Thanks, Sam."

I pulled on my own bottle and then leaned back on my elbows, searching the stars. They were so much brighter here. He leaned back next to me and followed my gaze.

"So, you're gay," he said bluntly after a few moments.

A surprised laugh burbled out of me and his chortle followed. "Bi," I corrected him.

"Ah. Is that weird?"

"No. Once I figured it out, it seemed like everything snapped into place. Like I solved a mystery I didn't know existed."

"Ah."

I glanced over at him and raised an eyebrow. "You're so loquacious, has anyone ever told you that?"

"I am a man of few, but always correct, words." He tipped his bottle toward me, giving me a lopsided grin. Silence settled around us again.

Sam cleared his throat and leaned forward to rest his forearms on his knees. "I thought I knew everything about you."

"I thought I knew everything about me, too. Surprise!" I spread my arms and did jazz hands.

He chuckled. "When do we get to meet Alex?"

I studied him for a moment. "I'm not sure yet."

"Well, if you're in love, and it's real, it better be sooner rather than later."

"You've all been really chill about this." I took another sip of my beer.

He looked at me like I'd suggested we run to the moon. "Yeah. Duh."

And that was that. He shrugged and put his arm around me. "We love you, little sister. There's nothing you could do that would stop that from being true. Certainly not falling in love. Sorry for all the heteronormativity all these years."

I pulled back, a look of astonishment on my face. "How do you know a word like heteronormativity?"

He responded gravely. "*Queer Eye*. Duh."

"You voluntarily watch *Queer Eye*?" I said skeptically but with mirth.

"Not at first. A girl I was dating loved it. But now I'm hooked."

I shook my head, smiling. "That is the cutest thing I have ever heard. My brother, the *Queer Eye* fan."

"Guess we'll always surprise each other, huh?"

A sadness coursed through me when I realized that I didn't even know what television shows my brother enjoyed. "We should talk more. Hang out when we can."

He clinked his bottle to mine. "Deal. And Paige, you know you'll always have a safe place to land with me, right?"

"Ditto."

§

When I arrived home, I unpacked, ordered sushi, and waited for Alex to arrive. When I heard the knock, I flung open the door and she was grinning in a way I'd never seen before, like she had the most delicious, juicy secret of her life.

"Well, they can't wait to meet you," I told her.

"'Course not, I'm fantastic."

"Come here, you." I pulled her inside and wrapped my arms around her in a long hug, which she returned. I could feel her heartbeat against my own chest and kissed her tenderly, letting it linger, until she pulled away.

I caught a weird faraway look in her eyes.

"What's up? Something's up." I pulled her by the hand to the loveseat, where she tangled her legs up with mine and laced her fingers through my hair.

"I have something to tell you."

My heart rate sped up considerably. I did not like where this was going.

"Spit it out." My words were clipped, my palms sweaty.

She sighed heavily and intertwined our fingers. "I'm leaving."

ELEVEN

I felt like I had been tasered. My hands were shaking and before I could stop them, my eyes filled with tears. In three seconds flat, I went from love and romantic bliss, the high of telling my family snapped away, and I felt a pang through my heart as though she had reached in and squeezed it into mush herself.

"What do you mean, leaving?" I gasped.

Alex, who had been looking down at our hands knotted together, looked up at me.

"On *tour*! I'm going on a tour! Oh my god, Paige, what did you think I meant?" She was half-laughing, half-shocked at my reaction and brought my hands up to her mouth. She kissed them. "I'm not leaving *you*."

The relief I felt coursed through my body, and I actually did start half-crying through laughter. Alex tenderly wiped the tears from my cheeks and we continued to chuckle at my reaction.

"So this is what you meant when you said you were dramatic," she said through her snickers.

"You can't fault me for that, all you said was you were leaving." I pouted.

She leaned over and claimed my lips with hers in a way that said she wasn't going anywhere. "I guess I just figured you would know what that means. I'm a touring comedian, so I'm leaving, to go on tour." She was still amused at my reaction.

I kept pouting and vaguely remembered her saying something like that on our first date. Then I realized that she was actually leaving. My lower lip jutted out further.

"Now I'm just sad that you're going. I'm happy for your tour, obviously, but I can't believe how much I'm going to miss you." I snuggled in closer to her. "When do you go?"

"Next week. It's a small Midwest tour with a couple of other queer lady comedians. We're calling it 'We're So Brave' and it's already sold out in a bunch of places. I'll be back at the end of August, in time to see you kill it at the concert. Then I'll be gone for another week or so."

I beamed. "Did you plan that around me?"

"Maybe." She smiled secretly at me and I stroked her bottom lip with my fingertip, touched.

"Why 'We're So Brave'?"

"It's a nod to how many dummies have told us how brave we are to be out *and* be women *and* be comedians. *So* brave of us to live our lives, you know?"

I chuckled. The name was perfectly her, subversive and clever. I trailed my fingers down her arm. "That's amazing. You're amazing. I'm so excited for you. And sad for me."

She looked down at me, a serene smile on her face. "I am also both of those things. I wish you could come with us."

"Me too."

We were interrupted by my buzzer. Our sushi had arrived. Over spicy tuna rolls, she told me all about her tour. She'd be all over the Midwest, including Nebraska, Iowa, Wisconsin, downstate Illinois, Indiana, and Ohio. I was impressed with the scale. I knew she was a rising star, but I didn't know she was going to play such large venues.

"I hope I never have to play in a tiny, seedy bar where no one pays attention ever again," she said when I told her that.

"I'm so proud of you." I clinked my can of grapefruit La Croix against hers.

She studied me for a moment, her gaze full of love and desire and all the ways I wanted to be seen. "I am so in love with you."

It was so simple. So sweet.

"It's going to be really difficult to... not be with you someday soon." She looked down at her plate, scattered with loose grains of rice.

"Let's cross that bridge when we come to it." I sounded much more sensible than I felt. I stacked the empty sushi containers and took our plates to the tiny sink. I heard her approach behind me and she wrapped her arms around my waist, her chin on my shoulder.

"Will you take care of Sammy while I'm gone?"

"Of course. I love that little nugget." I brushed a sponge over the plates and put them in the drying rack. She didn't move from behind me.

"Maybe you could just stay at my place. It's closer to the rehearsal studio anyway. And no offense, but this place leaves something to be desired." I could feel her lift her head and no doubt take in the tiny square: the bed in the corner, the love seat and coffee table which barely left room to walk between them and the TV stand.

"What are you talking about? This is a palace." Done with the dishes, I turned and wrapped my arms around her neck. "That's a very generous offer and I'd love to."

"I like knowing I'll be coming home to you."

"I like knowing you'll be coming home."

She pressed her lips to mine, her hands sneaking under my shirt and warming my whole body from the inside out. We made the most of the time we had.

§

"All right, my beauties, this is it. The first run through of Act One. Are you ready?" Our director, Andrea, was always enthusiastic, kind, and tough as nails. She was our leader for a reason, and I was beside myself to do her proud.

I took a deep breath. A first run through of the first act, off-book, and with the story finally set into place, was nerve wracking to me. This meant no stopping, no calling "Line!" when I forgot one, and powering through to get notes afterwards.

I was nervous, but confident in what we had achieved so far. Dev caught my eye from across the studio. He gave me a gigantic, goofy grin and an enthusiastic thumbs up. I winked at him.

"Places, please," our stage manager called.

Andrea settled in behind the folding table with the rest of the production team and whispered something to Toby. He looked down at his notebook and smiled secretly. This was what I loved about her: she was all about lifting us up and giving us the space to work out what we needed to. She wanted the show to be as incredible as she knew we could make it, and deriding people was not in her wheelhouse.

Positive reinforcement and giving us a clear understanding of what she wanted was what guided her.

I felt a rush of gratitude. I was the luckiest actor in history.

The musical starts out with a spectacular opening number, bringing us to Cassandra's fairytale-like kingdom with rich harmonies and incredible dancing. I wasn't in it, but I loved watching it every time. The whole cast was phenomenal and the first scene went without a hitch.

I entered in the second scene and suddenly felt it: the show had begun to live in my bones. Seeing all the pieces come together from the rehearsal process, seeing it all in order and coming to life, I fused with Cassandra, her optimism, and her underlying fierceness in the first act. I moved through the scenes with ease, embodying her, my clear voice ringing out when the doubts crept in about the future laid out for her.

The act ended with Cassandra taking charge of her life in a song called "I Am Standing". It was sure to become *the* song for aspiring musical theater kids to belt out in audition rooms in the coming years. An "On My Own", a "Fly, Fly Away", an "Astonishing", the kind of song that directors would be so sick of, they would include requests not to sing it in audition notices.

I loved it, every moment of it. The build, the belt, the key change. I performed the blocking from muscle memory, feeling Cassandra emerge through my every pore. The last note echoed through the room, a high belt at the end that I had only achieved with our vocal coach's assistance but could now perform with ease.

My eyes were closed. Silence fell. Two seconds passed... three...

...and the room exploded into applause. I opened my eyes and looked around at my castmates and the team, beaming. The clapping faded as the cast all hugged and collapsed together on the floor in front of the folding table.

Andrea stood up. "I cannot begin to tell you how excited I am. You've knit the show together beautifully, and I am thrilled."

We grinned around at each other, punching shoulders and smooching cheeks.

"But I do have notes, lots of them. After the break." We all groaned sarcastically and Andrea smiled down at us like we were her children. Which we kind of were.

"Let's take a ten," our stage manager said from the end of the table. We dispersed around the studio.

Toby motioned me over. "Join me for a trip to the vending machine?"

"Of course." I picked up my water bottle and followed him out of the studio and down the hall to the water fountain and snack machines. He put his card in and selected a series of candy bars.

I raised my eyebrows at him. His sugar addiction was amusing.

"I have a weakness," he sighed and grinned bashfully. He chose a treat and ripped open the package. He wandered over to the window at the end of the hallway, munching on his chocolate. I followed. Toby was a man of few words and I knew to wait for him to begin what he wanted to say.

We gazed out of the window together at the sunny Chicago day. I watched the El go by and could hear the rumble of the tracks.

Bluntly, he began, "I don't tell you this to hurt you in any way, so please don't take it that way."

I turned sharply to him, my stomach immediately turning to a ball of lead.

"No, it's good. Just prefaced with something that could be construed as unpleasant."

"Toby," I pleaded. "Just tell me."

He pocketed his other chocolate and returned his attention to the outdoors. "When I began writing this show, I didn't have anyone in mind for Cassandra. The three other ladies the team brought in for it would have done just fine. I think we can both acknowledge that."

I nodded, kind of guessing where this was going. "Jazzy Summers is a force to be reckoned with."

"That she is. But a week before the auditions started, I saw *Cabaret* and noticed you in the ensemble. You positively took my breath away. The way you commanded the stage and captured the eyes of the entire audience, even when you were in the back. You captivated me. When you had that little solo in the second act, I saw her. I saw Cassandra in you. And I knew you were it. I asked the team to bring you in right after the show.

"And I thought I would have to fight to have you, I really did. You know how new shows rely on names to bring people in. But when you came in, it was nearly unanimous from the start. We had to go through the rigmarole but... it was you all along."

My eyes had filled with tears. I had never heard Toby talk this much and what he was telling me were some of the nicest things anyone had ever said to me. My heart soared.

"Plus, in the end, we got Jeffrey, so we got our 'name.'" He paused to chuckle. Jeffrey Wright played Cassandra's father and was a legit Broadway legend. He had also starred in a long-running CBS series that was extremely popular, so he was a big enough name for the production team.

"Thank you, Toby. That means so much to me."

"That's not all." He grinned and pulled out his other candy bar. "Cassandra's story is mine, you know. She's a person who is slated for a life she doesn't want. And that was me. My dad expected me to take over his investment firm. I couldn't face it. After a year as a miserable business major upstate, I transferred to NYU, began playwrighting which I had always been passionate about, came out to my parents and everyone I knew, shocked my dad practically to death. But it was worth it in the end. He's very proud of me now."

I caught his eyes which were twinkling at me. I was rendered speechless.

"And you are doing Cassandra so much justice. This is as much your story as it is mine, and everyone's, in that room. I am so proud of you, and I wanted to thank you for bringing her to life. You are Cassandra. Please do not forget that."

A tear escaped and slid down my cheek. Toby laced his arm through mine and we continued to gaze at the city five stories below.

"You know when you asked me if it was okay for Cassandra to fall in love with a woman?"

Toby nodded.

"Well, literally that weekend I had started dating my first girlfriend."

A small, shocked *ha* escaped him. "How fortuitous."

"It was."

We stayed quiet for a few more moments. "This makes us friends for life, you know," he said.

"I know." I patted his hand and we turned to return to the studio.

§

"Honey, I'm home!" I called as I entered Alex's apartment. I dragged my suitcase in behind me and crouched down to pet Sammy when he swirled around my legs.

"I'm in here." Alex's voice came from her bedroom. Which was in total chaos.

Alex stood on the other side of her bed in just a tank and underwear, clothes strewn all over the bed, the dresser, and every other surface. Her hands on her hips, she raised her big doe eyes to me and gave me a look so plaintive I started to laugh.

I plucked a shirt from the bedside lamp and crossed to her side of the bed. "So what's going on here?"

"I think I forgot how to pack for a tour."

"Really? Couldn't tell."

She bumped her hip into mine and then collapsed onto all the clothes on the bed. Her voice was muffled when she said, "I don't wanna leave you."

I fell down next to her and she turned her head to meet my gaze. "You're not leaving me."

She sighed heavily. "I know, I know, and I'm really excited about this tour finally coming to fruition." She rolled over onto her back and stared at the ceiling. "But we have a limited time together anyway, and I don't want to lose an entire month or more."

I reached for her hand and pulled her close to me. She wrapped herself around me and buried her face in my neck.

"I understand completely. I don't want to lose the time either. Let's just say that absence makes the heart grow fonder and not think about it." I nudged her cheek with my nose, then softly kissed her when she turned her face to mine.

"You're being very practical." She sat up.

I glanced around the room at the chaos of Alex's entire wardrobe. Beginning to chuckle, I looked over at her. "One of us has to be."

She gave off a tinkling laugh and we set about organizing her tour clothes. I made sure she thought about everything she would need not just onstage, but lounging, traveling, sleeping, and going out.

"You're very good at this. It seems like every time I go out on a tour, I forget everything about the last time."

"I toured with *Rent* for over a year, so I remember it well."

She turned to me, one hand on her hip, a questioning look on her face. "You did?"

"Yeah, I understudied Maureen and went on at least once a week. I swear we've talked about this before but judging by the look on your face, we haven't."

"You know *Rent* was one of the most formative experiences of my life? I saw it on a tour in high school. I wanted to be, or do, Maureen."

"I had no idea a musical had a huge impact on you."

We had both paused, the crackling air electric between us. Many people our age had formative experiences with this particular show, and obviously it was very close to my heart. There was something in the air between us now, something that felt like we were meant to be.

I dropped Alex's gaze and went back to folding one of her t- shirts. I could still feel her looking at me, but then she went back to folding.

A few moments later, she said, "Hold up. You played Maureen."

"Yes." I wasn't sure where this was going.

"Maureen, the bisexual, who leaves Mark for JoAnne."

I paused my folding, looking off into the distance, the realization dawning. "Oh my god."

"How did you not know?" Alex threw a pair of jeans at me and doubled over, laughing so hard I saw tears glistening in her eyes.

I joined in, unable to believe it had taken me this long after that role to understand my sexuality. "I guess because I hadn't met you yet."

That stopped her laughter and she turned serious in an instant.

I moved over to her, took the shirt she was holding and tossed it into her case. I let my hands slide along the skin of her waist under her tank top. I slowly lowered the strap of her tank and kissed her shoulder tenderly. I heard her gasp a little as I moved my hands up the small of her back and pulled her shirt up and over her head. Gently, I laid her down on the bed, now clear of her clothes and pulled her underwear off.

She grasped the bottom of my top and pulled it up over my head. I swooped my shorts off as well, and then slid on top of her, our whole bodies touching. I could feel my skin tingling everywhere it met hers as we kissed for an eternity. Everything about Alex was soft and dreamy and I buried myself into worshipping every part of her. Her lips, her thighs, her breasts. I memorized every dip and curve in her body, wanting to remember the feel of her forever, not just while she was on tour, but after. When this was inevitably over.

As we both gasped for breath an hour later, contented and loved completely, she wrapped her arms around me and kissed my nose. "I love you."

"I love you, too."

"No matter what happens in the future, I am going to think of this perfect moment forever," she whispered.

"I will, too," I whispered back. Her lips met mine again and I wanted to stay in this moment for the rest of time. She was the one to break the spell.

"I should probably show you all the practical things about this place."

I sighed, not wanting the magic to be over, but knowing she was right.

We toured her apartment and she showed me everything I needed to know: all of Sammy's needs, the laundry room in the basement, the way to run the finicky dishwasher, where she kept spare batteries and lightbulbs, and all the other things I would need to know while I lived in her place.

The rest of the evening was spent watching mindless television until we decided to snuggle up in bed and talk.

We swapped stories about being in our twenties, and her first time at the gay clubs in Boystown. I regaled her with stories of being on tour with *Rent*. We spoke of our hopes and dreams and fears of the future of our careers, what we were passionate about, and how we wanted to spend our old age.

Sammy settled down between us at one point as we talked and kissed, and his purring lulled us both to sleep in the early morning hours.

Alex's blaring alarm startled us both awake and once our heart rates lowered, we met each other's eyes, both of us feeling pitiful for how much we'd miss each other. In the shower together, we didn't say a word, just soaped each other down and cherished our skin against skin.

After a piece of toast each, it was time for Alex to call her Lyft. I did not anticipate how sad I would be watching her go. I took her shoulder bag and she her suitcase out to the sidewalk and we stood facing each other, mirrored melancholic looks in our eyes. We stepped together simultaneously and hugged tightly. I pulled back and gazed into the warmth of her eyes and we both smiled.

Her soft lips were on mine when the car pulled up. She pulled away.

"Kick ass," I told her, my hands on her waist. "I know you will."

"You kick ass. I know *you* will. I'll call you when we get to Nebraska."

"Don't forget about me." I pulled her close again, put my hands to either side of her face and kissed her with intensity.

"Impossible," she said. Reluctantly, we both stepped away and put her bags in the popped trunk. She opened the back door and turned back just as she was about to climb in.

"I love you."

"I love you, too."

"See you in August."

I nodded. She climbed in the car and waved as it drove away.

Upstairs, Sammy greeted me with a chirp and hopped on the couch like he wanted me to sit next to him. I did, and he crawled into my lap without hesitation.

"I guess it's me and you, bud." He flopped down and accepted the scritches I gave him behind his ears.

It was going to be a long few weeks.

TWELVE

As I waited for Alex to return to Chicago, I was starting to feel the pressure of having a lead in a Broadway-level production. I took over the show's Instagram account for a day, I was on the phone with interviewers for *Playbill* and various Broadway resources online. Strategy meetings with the PR team left my head spinning.

It was a lot.

No one had warned me about the pressure I would feel as basically the face of the show. I just wanted to do my job and do it well, and that included all of this public relations stuff. I was grateful, but I was in a low-simmering constant state of anxiety, especially without Alex to help stave it off.

Costume fittings had begun in earnest and once Cassandra's Act One costumes were complete, I got to do a photo shoot during which I felt like a queen. For *Cabaret*, we had done a few shoots and promos, but it was nothing like having the lead. I wanted to project Cassandra's innocence and strength and hoped I'd impressed.

One week after Alex left, I walked into the studio, after having just finished our morning conversation. She had sounded tired and I felt a bit rushed off the phone, which was fine if that was the case, but it still unsettled me.

"Paige!" Toby almost screamed at me from across the room. I startled and dropped my bag in a chair. Everyone in mid-stretch, mid-coffee, mid-conversation turned to look at me. The room fell silent and my heart began to pound, especially after my conversation with Alex. Perhaps I'd said something wrong in one of the interviews. Maybe I had disparaged someone, but when I wracked my brain for whom or how, I couldn't come up with anything. I had only been positive in my conversations. Nevertheless, in those silent seconds, I was unnerved.

Then I saw Toby's face. And Andrea's. And the rest of the team behind the table, every single one of them, had huge grins on their faces. Toby, holding a tube in front of his chest, turned slowly, and looked right into my eyes. I felt myself begin to walk across the rehearsal room as he let the tube unfurl in front of him.

I gasped. It was a photo of me, but it was Cassandra who radiated out of the poster. My brown hair was given honey highlights and blown out, and it swirled around my made-up face, from which my hazel eyes burned with ambition and desire and passion. My mouth was set in an innocent, nearly imperceptible, upturned smile. The dress, a bit Greek goddess, a bit badass witch, was light blue fading to gray and black in an ombre pattern as it neared the floor. My arms were spread wide, my skin positively glowing, and the girl in the poster looked as though she were floating. *On Her Own* was emblazoned above my wild hair, and in the corner were the performance dates and the name of the theater. Our closing night would be New Year's Eve.

There it was, officially. Alex and I had an end date. I shoved that thought aside immediately and tried to enjoy this moment, the here and now. I was ninety-nine percent successful.

I had never felt so gorgeous in all my life, but also completely outside of my body. I couldn't quite believe this goddess was me. And if this is who I was projecting onstage--I went ahead and let myself think it--this show was going to be a *hit*.

The graphics department and photographer deserved several awards.

The conversations around the room swirled around me, suddenly increasing in volume as if I had been underwater. I came back to myself and looked around at all the smiling faces, snippets of conversations coming at me.

"...complete goddess..."

"...utterly gorgeous..."

"This show is going to shine."

"...had no idea it was going to be so powerful..."

I felt pats on the back and Dev's arm around my shoulder as we all excitedly took in the first piece of the show really brought to life. We'd been in the studio for so long and were eager to get into the theater and onto the real set. It got boring using the various wood blocks and plain doors that made up the rehearsal set pieces. I wanted to get into Cassandra's palace and her chambers and the coven's woods. I wanted to feel that poster for real, which I knew I would the moment we stepped onto the stage.

"All right, everyone, calm down. We're all pleased we have a goddess in our midst," Andrea said to us as we chittered and giggled and danced around. She wore an affectionate smile and I winked at her.

"We *are* very lucky to have you, goddess," I said. She rolled her eyes at me as everyone cheered for her. But she was still smiling.

"I want to do a full run through today, because sitz probe is next week, and we are going to be working on the songs with the orchestra."

A frisson of excitement ran through the room. A sitz probe, when we would sing with the orchestra for the first time, was always magical. The arrangements were going to be gorgeous, and I couldn't wait to hear our songs with more than just the piano and drums.

After we'd run through the first few scenes of Act One, we were given a union break. I approached Toby. "So when can I share that glorious poster?"

He grinned. "I believe the rollout starts today. I'll see if I can get you the hi-res files."

I squeezed his arm and he went off, to get more candy bars, presumably.

After a grueling rehearsal, we all took the El down to the Cadillac Palace Theater, where our show would be open before, hopefully, making the move to Broadway. The posters had been installed that day. The sun was beginning to go down in that late summer way, casting the tops of the buildings in pink and throwing shadows along LaSalle Street.

We stood across the street from the theater, gazing up at the magnificent, vintage Cadillac Palace sign. The marquee below had "*On Her Own*: Opening October 22nd" spelled out in those giant black letters. And below the marquee, under the globe lights, were posters of Cassandra.

Of me. The world took on a shimmery quality, cementing this moment into my heart.

My breaths came in gasps as I took in the totality of what was happening: my literal dreams, the ones I'd had since I was a child, were coming true. Intellectually, I had known this, of course. But it didn't sink in until I saw my face on those posters at the theater in which I would perform. I bit my bottom lip and let the tears fall, not feeling foolish in the slightest. My castmates stood around me, arms around each other, my family here in Chicago. Dev laid his head on my shoulder and Steph grasped my hand, our palms sweaty. My friends were teary, too. We all were.

After a few moments, Dev straightened up and pulled out his phone. As if on cue, we all did the same, snapping some pics from far away. I knew our Instagrams were going to blow up tonight. Like a litter of excited puppies, we tripped our way across the street and took various pictures of the marquee and the posters.

"Come on, Paige, just stand next to yourself!" Dev tried to convince me that I should take a picture with the poster. I shook my head.

"No way, that is way too egotistical."

Dev gave me a murderous look. "This could be your only lead ever, girl, get over there."

I snorted at his vote of confidence. "Not yet. Maybe later."

He rolled his eyes. "Fine, but if that were me, I would stand around it all day hoping to get recognized."

"Of course you would." I slung my arm around him and kissed his cheek. My castmates were taking turns posing with the poster, and that was enough for me. Around us, we could feel the excitement and anticipation of putting our show in front of a crowd. The magic of taking them to another place. The magic of live theater.

§

On the train home, I texted Alex the photos of the poster and the marquee. She called me as I walked up the stairs and into her apartment. Sammy began scolding me for not being home sooner to give him dinner.

"I cannot believe that's my *girlfriend*," Alex was saying as I opened a can of cat food. Sammy twirled around my legs, yelling at me to go faster.

"I can't believe Sammy is this demanding."

"Don't change the subject. You look incredible. I mean, it's you, you always look incredible, but this... This is really something."

"It feels real now." I set the dish on Sammy's food mat and he went to town, gobbling it down before Alex had her next sentence out.

"Forgive me for this, but my only real theater experience has been community, like what I've been around the most. I've seen Broadway shows, but I just kind of-- I don't know. I had it in my head that you would be in front of Western Springs Players with a hundred people in the audience? I'd never considered the scale of this, I guess. That's not insulting, is it?"

I smiled to myself. I completely understood where she was coming from. "I totally get it. I keep thinking 'Oh, I'm in the school play', but now..."

"It's huge."

"Hopefully, it sells out most nights. Then I'll be in front of two thousand of my closest friends every evening."

"I'm so proud of you." Her voice rang with sincerity. A comfortable silence fell between us and a rush of gratitude flowed through me for her unending support. In that moment, I missed her so much I thought I would cry.

"Thank you. When are you coming home?"

"I'll be back for the concert."

"Yes, but then leaving again."

"I'll be back in for good in September." Her voice was a little sad, the huskiness a little more prominent. My phone trilled and I pulled it back from my ear. She was FaceTiming me. I smiled and accepted.

She was curled up on a hotel bed, a generic painting of a tree behind her. "Greetings from Iowa's finest Days Inn."

"I can only imagine the glory. It's so good to see your face. I love your face." I settled down onto her sofa and Sammy hopped up onto the back of it, presumably so he could see her properly.

Alex's face lit up and she brought the phone closer to her face. "Hey, Sammy boy! I miss you so much."

Completely adorable. Sammy settled in for a nap behind me, barely pricking up an ear. I chuckled.

"Well, at least you're happy to see me," Alex said, her mouth set in a cute pout. "I love your face, too." She collapsed back onto the pillows and held the phone above her face.

We let a few seconds pass just looking at each other. Trepidation filled me for a moment before I asked, "Are we going to talk about it?" I wondered if she'd thought about the end date of the show. Of us.

She frowned, a wrinkle forming between her eyebrows. "New Year's Eve?"

"Yeah."

I watched as she made a big production of thinking very hard, scrunching up her face, hemming and hawing. I was already laughing when she answered. "No. Not yet."

"Fine by me. How's the tour going?"

"You know, for a bunch of queer ladies in small Midwestern towns, we're selling out and we've only had like, two instances of homophobia."

I huffed, feeling protective. But if she wasn't going to make it an issue, I wouldn't either. "Impressive, I guess. Are you having fun?"

She gave me a soft smile, one I knew was just for me. One that not a lot of other people have seen on her face, a mix of love and longing and perfect contentment. "I am, but I'm really missing you. This is much harder than I anticipated. And don't get me wrong, I love a good FaceTime, and I *really* loved Sunday night."

I waggled my eyebrows at her, remembering our first foray into phone sex.

Her tone turned serious. "But it's really hard not being with you. It's only been a few months and I am so completely in love with you and I don't know how we're supposed to say goodbye at the end of this thing. I can't leave Chicago, and I know you can't stay, and it just seems impossible that we have to break up when you feel like the biggest part of my life."

The words seemed to spill out of her, unplanned and beautiful but painful to hear.

"I don't know, Paige. I just really love you and I need you to know how much."

We gazed at each other through the screens for a few long moments, and I wanted more than anything in the world to feel her soft lips against mine, to hold her close and tell her we'd never have to part.

Which was ludicrous since we already were apart.

"I'm with you completely," I told her instead. "And until we have to, I'm not leaving you. Not possible."

"Maybe we'll never have to." The hope in her voice was unmistakable.

"Maybe."

It seemed we were making the promise that lovers since the dawn of time had been making to each other, no matter how unlikely or impossible: we would never have to part, not really. We can make it work. It will be different for us.

We talked late into the night about lighter things. At nearly two in the morning, we went quiet at the same time. I gazed at her sweet face and stroked a finger down my phone, wishing I could feel her silky skin against mine. A thought entered my head that I wasn't sure I could say aloud. A thought that, if I told her, might scare her off.

I wanted to stay with her forever.

In a voice on the verge of sleep, she read my mind and said, "Paige, I know it's impossible, but if I could hold you forever, I would."

I inhaled deeply. "I want that more than you'll ever know."

She sighed heavily, content, and her eyes fluttered closed.

"Goodnight, Alex. I love you."

"Always," she mumbled.

I hung up the phone and rolled over in her sheets, facing the moon outside the window, our words churning in my mind. Always. Forever.

How desperately I wanted to believe in forever.

§

The next Monday, I stepped out of the elevator and was greeted by the sounds of oboes and violins tuning, of drums intermittently being hit. The day of the sitz probe had finally arrived. As I walked into the studio, I could feel the hum of excitement from the cast and crew and my stomach flitted in delicious anticipation. This was a really special moment for any show, but finally hearing original music being played by a twenty-piece orchestra was truly unique. I knew I was experiencing something relatively few people had.

The rehearsal studio had been transformed into an orchestra pit with chairs around the perimeter. All of the musicians were sitting or standing in a semi-circle in the middle of the room, their music stands at various heights. A clarinetist played a run. A tuba bellowed from the other side of the room.

Toby gestured for me to sit by Steph and Jeremy near the team's folding table, set up facing the orchestra. I walked over, smiling nervously at them both, and set my bag in a chair next to Jeremy. Toby waved a short, serious, redheaded woman over. She held a baton in her hand.

"Paige, this is Marta. She's our conductor."

I shook her hand, trying not to wither under her intense gaze. "Nice to meet you, Marta. I'm so excited for all of this to come together."

At this, her expression softened. "I am, too. Please watch me for cues." She walked away.

I turned to Toby, a questioning look on my face.

"She's strict, but she's a genius. She'll guide us in the right direction."

"I don't doubt it," I said. I sat down and took my score out of my bag. While I had memorized it, it was best to be prepared.

Andrea stood at a mic next to the conductor's stand. The rest of the cast had arrived and were sitting in the chairs along the perimeter of the room.

"Well, folks," Andrea said into the mic. She jumped a little bit at the sound of her voice echoing around the room and we all gave off a bit of nervous laughter. The air was charged with anticipation and nerves and excitement. "This is it. We are going to run through all the music from beginning to end today, and then make any necessary tweaks. We've also decided what song we'll be doing for the Broadway in Chicago concert at the end of the month."

Everyone in the room seemed to lean forward at once, as if hoping they would all get the chance to be on the Pritzker Pavilion stage.

"We've all decided that the best song to perform, logistically and emotionally, will be 'I Am Standing'."

She let the moment sink in. I glanced around at my castmates and noted their disappointment before realizing what this meant: I would be standing on that vast stage in front of thousands and thousands of people, alone.

My hands began to shake. Jeffrey patted my shoulder kindly. "Don't worry, kid," he whispered. "I did a solo on that stage years ago. You're going to be fine. More than fine. You're a star."

I gave him a shaky smile, feeling dozens of people eyeing me around the room. Andrea cleared her throat again.

"Paige, I know it's a big ask, but we're looking forward to you bringing down the house."

Someone began to clap--Dev, probably--and everyone else joined in. I breathed out through my nose and tried not to let the nerves get the best of me.

"Now, let's get down to business," Andrea called as the spontaneous applause died down. She nodded at Marta, who raised her baton. The musicians all readied their instruments. Marta brought her baton down and the orchestra began to play the overture.

I was immediately swept into the rich score, so much so that I forgot about my upcoming performance. Jeffrey and I sang our humorous duet, Dev led the company in the biggest numbers, and at the end of Act One, I stepped up to the mic to sing "I Am Standing". I turned the music stand to best see Marta, set my music on it, and gave her a nod. She nodded back, raised her baton, and suddenly I wasn't there.

Cassandra roared through me, taking her power back, deciding to live on her terms, and before I knew it, I belted out the last note and thunderous applause rained through the room. We had all been respectful during the music, quietly watching each number and taking our place next to Marta when needed. Now that Act One was over, and it had gone smoothly, the tension broke and we all fell about each other, giggling and shouting compliments. The stage manager called for our union break and I was congratulated by my castmates. Whatever they had been feeling about being denied the opportunity to perform at the concert, it had melted away.

Even Marta looked at me approvingly.

Over the crush of my cast, these beautiful weirdos I had come to love desperately, I glanced over at Toby, where he sat at the table.

His eyes were swimming with tears and pride. It seemed he couldn't do any more than he did: a simple thumbs up and a nod. I felt my own tears well up and nodded back.

We were ready to take on the world.

THIRTEEN

Concert day. I was a bundle of nerves for two reasons. One, I was singing in front of thousands of people, a song they'd never heard from a musical they'd never seen, and it was my job to make them want to. And two, Alex was coming home for the day. She and the other comedians on the tour had to cross through Chicago on their way downstate, so they had a day to crash in their own beds before moving on.

I had been given the day off of rehearsal so I could wrap my head around what I was doing tonight. The concert started at six and I had to be backstage and in hair and makeup by 5:30 p.m. I would sing last.

That was fine. I was fine. This was all *fine*.

It was just after ten when first, Sammy bolted from the kitchen to the front door. Then, I heard Alex's keys jangle in the lock. I ran after the cat and flung the door open before she could.

We stood and beamed at each other before she threw herself in my arms. Finally, I felt her soft lips on mine, tender at first, then fiercer. More urgent. She tasted of cherries and sunshine and I never wanted it to end. But Sammy was protesting that I was getting the first bit of affection and we tore ourselves away. Alex scooped Sammy up and smooshed her face into the fur on his neck.

"I missed you too, you little monster." Immediately, Sammy had had enough and squirmed to be put down. I watched this exchange with a deep affection for Alex running through me, the golden thread tightening for this woman who loved her cat as much as she loved me.

Well, maybe she loved me a little more.

She turned back to me as Sammy walked away from her, holding his tail high as if to say *You didn't need to come home, you know. I was fine without you.*

"Hi." I was still grinning, the sight of her making my heart go all gooey.

"Hi." She grinned back, but there was something behind her eyes I couldn't decipher. She stepped toward me and pulled me to her, our foreheads touching. "It's been a rough few weeks."

I nodded. "I really missed you." Our eyes met and that look was still there. Something she was guarding. My brow furrowed. "What is it?"

She pulled away from me, an inquisitive look on her face. "What is what?"

"Something's wrong."

She tilted her head, her expression saying *Search me.* "Nothing. I'm just completely--to be British about it-- knackered."

This was clearly all in my head. I crossed to the door and dragged her suitcase inside, closed, and locked it. I turned to her. "Well, then. We better get you to bed."

A smile crept across her face and we ran to the bedroom, shirts and shorts littering the hallway as we went. I buried myself in her softness and cherished every kiss. Touching her again was the breath of fresh air I needed to calm me down. Her every movement, her delectable moans, brought me back to myself. Brought me back home.

After I eased my nerves on Alex in the most delicious way, we went for a late lunch. Afterward I began to get ready for the concert. She would be joining Dev and Steph and the rest of the cast and crew in the seats at stage left, so she didn't need to leave as early as I did. Unfortunately, my cousin's wedding was the same weekend, so my family were sad they couldn't be there. I promised them a video.

At the door, as I was about to leave, Alex wrapped her arms around me in an incredibly warm hug, then pulled back and gazed at my face. She still had that unsettled, guarded look in her eye, but there was love there, too.

"Paige Parker, you are going to knock the socks off of every single person in that park tonight. And beyond that, on stage every night, and beyond that on Broadway. Every. Single. Night." She placed her warm palm on the side of my face and I nuzzled into it. "You are the most magnificent woman who has ever existed. Just do everything you've always done, and you'll bring down the house."

I brought my hand up to hers and squeezed. I kissed the inside of her wrist. She gave me a look full of love, and I could feel my heart beat faster. Together, we stepped closer until the entire length of our bodies were touching. She touched her lips to mine in a kiss so tender and sweet, my knees actually went weak, which I didn't know happened in real life. I pulled back, a soft smile playing on my lips.

"I love you."

"I love you, too." She kissed me one more time, lingering a moment before pulling away. "Now get outta here. Go be the superstar that you are."

I picked up my bag, gave her one more peck on the cheek and trotted down the stairs, feeling lighter than air.

§

The concrete area behind the stage had none of the glamour of the stage itself. I waited in the wings and listened to the other performers before me, trying to calm my nerves and breathe through my nose.

In the tiny, bare dressing room I'd been given, I had done my hair, though not as expertly as it was done during the photoshoot, and my makeup was set. The false eyelashes made me feel like a total powerhouse. My dresser, Sunny, had zipped and pinned me into the first act dress, adjusted my mic pack, and I'd made my way to the wings.

Andrea was reading over her notecards. As the last notes of the song faded, she sidled up to me, took my hand, and squeezed it. "You are everything we wanted in Cassandra, Paige. I have every faith that you are going to bring every single person out there to their knees."

I squeezed her hand back, unable to say anything. God, I hoped she was right. She was introduced and stepped onto the stage. I closed my eyes, barely listening to her introduction to this brand-new musical, until I heard my name.

"Please welcome Paige Parker, singing 'I Am Standing' from *On Her Own*, a new musical from Toby Anderson."

The next breath I took was Cassandra's. While the audience applauded for my entrance, I strolled across the warm wood floor of the stage right to center. In one second, looking beyond the stage lights, I took in the view in front of me before I tried to erase it from my mind completely.

Millennium Park was vast and bathed in the light of early summer evening, not quite dusk. In front of me, eager faces were all trained toward me in the rows and rows of red seats under the steel crisscross beams of Pritzker Pavilion. Beyond the auditorium seating, the grass seemed to stretch for miles. It seemed like all of Chicago was there, sitting on blankets, pouring wine into plastic cups, and stuffing themselves with cheese. The summer breeze touched my bare skin and I gave an almost inaudible sigh, all in this one second.

It would have overwhelmed me had I dwelled on it. But I was Cassandra, who wasn't going to let anything rattle her anymore.

Behind me, the pianist gave me my note, and then the orchestra began the song's intro. I closed my eyes and sang, the verses becoming more confident, more determined, until we hit the key change in the latter third and I ended the song decisively with the belted high *A*.

Feeling victorious, I opened my eyes and lived in a split second of silence, during which I thought maybe I'd failed. Or that it had all been a dream. Then a thunderous applause began, the cheering reaching my ears from the back of the park all the way to the front row. I glanced over to the seats at stage left and saw Alex, Dev, Steph, and all of my castmates standing and yelling out support for me. Alex, I noted, had tears tracing down her cheeks and her smile hit me like a sunbeam.

I exited stage right on a cloud. I had never felt like this before in my life. I had sung for crowds before, big ones, but never like this. Never in that capacity. I felt powerful, like I could take on anything. As Sunny helped me out of my costume, I felt my throat catch and tears spring to my eyes.

Andrea appeared in the dressing room as I was slipping into my sandals. I could hear the crowd mutely before she shut the door behind her. She leaned back against it and regarded me with such pride, the tears in my eyes began to fall.

"Oh, Paige." She came to me and wrapped me in a warm hug. I let the tears slide down my cheeks and relished this moment with this woman who had helped me bring Cassandra to life. "I am so proud of you."

"That was the best moment of my life," I mumbled into her shoulder.

She chortled and pulled back. "You take this moment into every performance, and we are going to have not only a hit Broadway show, but a superstar on our hands."

A knock on the door broke our embrace and I said, "Come in."

Toby poked his head around the corner and stepped inside while I was wiping my eyes. He didn't need to say anything. He just embraced me and I could feel the gratitude coming off of him in waves.

"Did I do you justice?" I whispered in his ear.

He just squeezed me tighter.

We wound our way out of the maze of concrete until we found ourselves back in the Loop and at the bar we'd designated as our meeting place.

A cacophony of sound greeted us as we made our way to our group. They cheered and clinked their glasses and bottles and generally made themselves nuisances to the entire establishment.

I loved them so hard.

I was caught up in a dozen hugs and accolades poured in from all around. Someone thrust a gin and tonic into my hand as I was accosted by everyone in the cast. While I accepted their compliments as graciously as I could--I didn't want to sound egotistical, but I had definitely nailed it--I looked around for Alex.

She sat at a table near the back of our group, watching me hug and kiss all of my castmates, pride in her eyes and a wide smile on her face. After five minutes, I finally extricated myself and made my way over to her. She stood up off her stool, her expression full of wonder and devotion. I pulled her to me and we kissed softly. Her arms wrapped around me in a tight hug, which I returned. I felt so grateful to have her in this moment with me, I almost started to cry. Again.

After a few moments, she said, "I am in awe of you. You are my hero. I love you."

I just squeezed tighter, and then I felt moisture on my shoulder. She was crying. Pulling back, I caressed the side of her face and asked her without words what was wrong.

She shook her head. "In every single sense of the word, you are awesome."

We were interrupted by Dev, who had climbed onto a stool and was clinking a fork against his cocktail glass.

"If you fall and break something, I will never forgive you," Andrea called as the chatter around us died down.

"I'll dance with a cast on for you, girl," Dev said.

Andrea shook her head but she was smiling.

Dev beamed at all of us and raised his glass. "A toast! I've known Paige for many years. I've known her through ups and downs and church basement theaters, through nine-hour Equity auditions, drunken Soho nights, through boyfriends and girlfriends." He paused and winked at Alex.

She laced her fingers through mine.

"I've known her through some drama, I've known her through some love. I've known her through moving across the country. And now we all get the privilege of being in this incredible show--thank you, Toby, Andrea--and we get to watch this woman's star rise. Paige, you were magnificent tonight and you are going to shine once we open."

He looked right into my eyes, "...it's us, baby, who are the lucky ones."

At this Maureen quote from *Rent*, my heart soared. I had said that line on my first tour out of college so many times, and it felt like everything had come full circle. "To Paige!" rang out from my show family and from Alex next to me, who still held my hand.

The revelry that night was unmatched by any I'd experienced in Chicago thus far, with the exception, perhaps, of the foam party on Pride. Alex was by my side for the whole of it, but she remained pretty quiet all night. Though I had the sensation that something was up since I'd seen that look in her eyes when she arrived home, I tried to chalk it up to the fact that we talked about the show all night and she didn't have a lot to add.

In the quiet Lyft ride home from the Loop, with Alex's soft hand in mine, I enjoyed watching the city lights go by. I hadn't drunk as much as I'd thought. In fact, I was feeling pretty sober and looking forward to curling up in bed with Alex and sleeping until noon. She would be leaving the next day, early evening. Maybe we could have a huge homemade brunch. I could make her bacon and my famous pancakes, the only thing I cooked well, and then perhaps we could do naughty things with syrup.

"Paige?" Alex nudged me. I must have dozed off because we were in front of her building already. I chuckled low to myself and opened the car door. We thanked the driver and I followed Alex up to her apartment.

Once inside, I set my bag down on the floor and turned to close and lock the door. I stretched my arms above my head and turned, yawning. "What do you think of a huge breakf--"

Alex was staring at me and her expression was absolutely wrecked. Her eyes were wide and sparkling with tears. She was looking at me like she was about to ship off to sea and never see me again. Her mouth was downturned, her lips trembling.

My whole body began to hum with anxiety. "Alex, what's--" I was rendered speechless, wanting to go to her but somehow unable to move.

She was silent for a few more moments, which felt like an eternity. Finally, her words came out in a gasp.

"I can't do this, Paige."

FOURTEEN

Ice flowed through me, freezing me in place. My hands began to shake. I couldn't compute the night I'd just had with the moment I was currently living in. Something was wrong with the universe, someone had flipped a switch and turned it upside down.

Alex's face was screwed up in a way I'd never seen but I couldn't make myself go to her. My brain just couldn't understand what was going on. We stood silently as the words she'd just uttered cut through the space between us. Our fragile relationship, as much as I had wanted to believe it was solid, shattered like glass.

Abruptly, she gasped and walked over to the couch, collapsing on it, her body racked with sobs. She doubled over, burying her face in her hands, my sweet pixie blonde, clearly feeling an immense amount of pain that I didn't know if I could do anything about.

Still frozen, I choked out, "Alex, what do you mean?"

Through her sobs, she reached her hand out to me, as if gesturing for me to come to her, but I couldn't. It was as though a barrier had gone up, a wall of her words between us. She groaned and more tears streamed down her cheeks.

"Please, just tell me what's going on," I choked out. I stood at the doorway, numb and blindsided.

It was as if I'd opened a floodgate. The words came tumbling out of her.

"Oh god, I didn't think that would come out of me tonight, but I couldn't keep it in any longer. I love you so much, I love you so, so much, in a way I have never loved anyone before but I don't know how to do this, how to make this work, I--" She took another gasping breath. Hearing her declaration of love gave me the ability to move. I slowly walked over to the couch and sank down beside her.

She wouldn't meet my eyes. I couldn't wrap my mind around the elation I had just been feeling and the completely contradictory emotions Alex had seemingly been having all night.

"I'm so sorry, I'm just so sorry, Paige, but I can't do this anymore."

All I could manage to say was, "Why?"

Alex stared forward at the blank television screen and I could see her take deep breaths, trying to stymie her tears.

I could feel her pain slicing through my chest and wanted to pull her into my arms to comfort her. But I remained as I was, frozen on the couch next to her, mind boggled.

"I am so sorry I'm doing this right after the concert and so close to your opening. You were incredible tonight. I have never been so enamored, so impressed, with anyone in my life. You commanded that whole stage, that whole park. It was truly the best performance I've ever seen. You were captivating and I want you to know that I am so proud of you, so proud to know you.

"That conversation we had, those promises of forever, I meant them, emotionally. I don't think that I will ever stop loving you. I don't think that's possible. But when I was gone, being away from you, and knowing how much of our lives would be *about* being away from each other. My heart broke without you, Paige."

She had stopped sobbing, but this was all the more heartbreaking. Silent tears streaked down her cheeks as she tried and failed to make me understand what she was thinking.

"But I just can't see how we're going to make this work. I just can't."

Silence fell and the reality of what she was saying crashed down around me. She turned her face to the ceiling, her tears finally abating. I felt the ice in my veins crack and flow through me, melting into despair.

We were doomed. From the start.

My eyes filled with tears and I let them fall, felt them run down my cheeks and splash onto my fingers. I let my gaze meet Alex's and felt a hurt so deep she may as well have punched me in the stomach.

"You're breaking up with me." My voice was hoarse somehow, nearly a whisper.

Alex bit her lip and nodded, then shook her head. Then she nodded again.

"I don't understand. Please help me understand." I felt helpless, lost.

She shook her head again and worried her bottom lip. I could tell she was trying to find the words as she took two deep breaths. Her eyes finally met mine. "If we get into this any deeper, you know how hard it's going to be to say goodbye when the show closes and you move back to New York. I'm doing this for us."

She turned away again and laughed absurdly. "God, that sounds so high and mighty. But I am. If we don't break up now, it's going to be much too hard to do on New Year's Eve. Winter is already hard enough."

I shook my head in disbelief. "But we were going to make the most of the time we had." My voice was small, like a child's, like I was begging to go on a school trip rather than pleading to keep the love of my life from destroying everything we'd built in these last few months. "We promised. We made promises, Alex."

Another tear ran down Alex's cheek. She brushed it away. "I wanted to believe we could promise that."

I huffed out an indignant breath. I thought we could. The tinge of regret in her voice cut me deeply.

A few tense moments passed silently. I felt betrayed, a little by her, but mostly by myself. I had promised I wouldn't come to Chicago and fall in love. That I would take the time for me. But here I was. I couldn't blame her for this.

Neither of us had expected our love to deepen so quickly, and I wanted it just as badly as she had. I thought we would be able to say goodbye when the time came, possessing the knowledge that it would be hard.

"I don't know how to move forward without you." I felt the truth of this statement deep inside me. I was never going to be the same. This would be my life now: before Alex and after Alex.

She hitched a leg up, mirroring my pose, and finally turned her face to mine. Our knees touched and she tentatively reached out to take my hand. I let her. She stroked her thumb over my palm, over the lifeline, and in the next three seconds, I watched our whole relationship flash by at the front of my mind, like a movie montage. The meeting, the first kiss, watching her onstage, the Cubs game, Pride, all the little moments laughing in bed and playing with Sammy. All of the love I felt flow from her to me and back again.

The golden thread was unraveling.

I couldn't believe this was happening. I flashed back to that night on FaceTime when we'd made all of our promises and frowned.

"I don't think this is right." I said slowly. Nothing about this felt right. And I was going to fight for it. "This isn't how this is supposed to happen. We're going to figure this out. I know we will. I am more connected to you than I have been to anyone in my life. We can find a way to make this work." I was pleading, deeply desperate in a way I had never felt, not with anyone.

Alex took another deep breath. "There's something I haven't told you."

I sucked in a breath and held it.

"I might move to L.A."

Her sad eyes met my surprised ones as I let out the breath. I slowly brought my hand away from hers and I watched her watch that happen. She closed her eyes as if she couldn't bear to see me pull away.

My words came out in almost a hiss. "What do you mean? How could you not have mentioned it?"

She couldn't look at me and ran her thumb over her lips. Her gaze fell downward and her voice was shaky. "I wasn't sure about anything. My agent sent my writing samples out and we've been getting some feedback. Shows are staffing for pilot season and I have a couple that are interested in meeting with me. In fact, one of them is almost guaranteed as long as the creator and I get along."

She put her palms over her eyes, rubbing them as she talked. "The whole time we've been together, I've had it in my head that I could possibly move to New York, you know? It's not an impossibility. I don't want to leave Chicago, but to follow you, to just *be* with you..." She dropped her hands and met my gaze, intense. "I'd go anywhere. I kept it at the back of mind. I might have."

Stunned, I sat forward, closer to her, feeling the loss of this unexpected possibility. "You might have?"

Nodding, she took my hands in hers, and once again, I let her. I squeezed her fingers. She squeezed back.

"I thought it wasn't impossible. And as long as it wasn't impossible, I wanted to keep being with you. But now, you're going to New York in a few months. And there's an eighty percent chance I'll be going to L.A. And there will be an entire country between us. I don't see how we can reconcile that." Silence fell. Her thumb traced my palm.

I glanced down at our intertwined hands. I came to my senses a bit. Had she told me that she would have moved to New York sooner, this would be even more soul crushing than it already was. I'm glad she hadn't. And what she was saying made sense now.

But I hated it, every second.

"So you think that it will just be easier to let it go now."

"I do," she whispered.

"'Easier' is doing a lot of work there." I chuckled sadly and she joined in, melancholy settling over the moonlit living room.

"It was never going to be easy, but with everything that's about to be going on for you, and my flying back and forth from L.A. now..."

I closed my eyes, willing myself to be in another time, another place, when Alex and I could be together and it wouldn't be complicated.

"I hate this." My voice was low, resigned.

"Me, too."

"I hate you just a little bit for making me see the sensibility of it. And for keeping L.A. from me." I snuck a glance at her face. She winced at my words, but her eyes were full of understanding.

"Me, too." She was quiet for a few more moments. "Would it be selfish of me to ask if we could have tonight?"

I gazed up at her in surprise. She cupped her hand gently around my chin and I felt a shaky smile cross my face. "Not at all." In unison, we entangled ourselves on the couch. Our foreheads touched and I brushed my nose on hers. She pressed her lips to mine, and I grasped her to me, as close as possible. I wanted this night together to be memorable.

We both knew it would be the last.

After a few minutes of her sweet kisses, she disentangled us and led me to the bedroom. We both stripped off our clothes then lay down, gazing at each other's bodies. I stroked my finger down her shoulder, her rib cage, the slope of her waist, her smooth thigh. I gazed at every freckle, every scar, every part of her. And I knew she was doing the same.

Moving over to me, she wrapped her legs around me and our hands explored every inch of each other. I was trying to memorize every part of her, every gasp, every sigh, every caress. As we brought each other to release, I gazed into her eyes, dancing in the moonlight, and she brought her lips to mine, burning with a fervor and a longing that I knew I would never be able to replicate.

We clung together, the entire length of our bodies touching. To me, we felt like a unit, so perfectly fit no one could ever tear us apart.

Except her, I guess.

Alex tucked her face into the crook of my neck and murmured, "I love you. That will never change."

"I love you," I said into the darkness. I felt her relax around me as she drifted to sleep, and I was content to lie there holding her until the sun began to turn the sky pink outside of the window.

I must have fallen asleep around dawn, because I woke up to the smell of bacon wafting into the bedroom. I pulled on Alex's silk robe and wandered to the kitchen. She was at the stove wearing only an apron, flipping pieces of bacon in a pan. It smelled amazing and I realized I was ravenous. I guess this was the last time she would cook breakfast for me in the nude. I smiled softly, searing the image into my brain.

I couldn't believe this was over. I couldn't believe this magnificent woman in front of me was about to be out of my life. She turned to me with a smile that held a trace of sadness behind it. I felt it too.

"Dangerous to cook bacon naked, no?" I said as I wrapped my arms around her from behind and kissed her temple.

"Hello," she said petulantly, and gestured with the tongs. "Apron."

I chuckled into her shoulder and then pulled away. I gathered the ingredients for pancakes and whipped up a batch quickly. We chatted about mundane things. A conversation she'd had with her mom, something goofy Dev had done at rehearsal. We sat down to pancakes and bacon at her kitchen table, and a flash of fresh pasta and garlicky kisses flew through my mind.

After pouring on a generous helping of syrup, Alex cut a pancake with the side of her fork. Just before raising it to her mouth though, she set it back down.

"I hope this is okay to say, but I'd still really love to come to the opening."

Pain clenched around my heart. I hadn't thought of that. "Of course it is. I want you to be there. It'll be hard but I can't imagine doing it without you in the audience, to be honest."

Relief crossed her expression. "Good. I wouldn't miss it for the world." She shoved the pancake in her mouth and chewed.

"Oh man," she moaned. "How am I just now finding out that my gi-- That you're an amazing pancake-maker?"

I smiled sadly, trying to brush past the fact that I wasn't her girlfriend anymore. She mirrored my expression and took my hand in her own for a moment.

Later, as Alex showered, I gathered all my things and packed my suitcase. Over breakfast, we had discussed me staying in her place to care for Sammy, but I ultimately decided it would be too hard. She had found another friend to come stay with him.

If we were going to break up, then we were going to do a clean break. I didn't want to have any hope that she would come back from tour or her upcoming trips to L.A. declaring how stupid this was and of course she would move to New York and she loved me and would I marry her.

I was still going to hope that, of course. I had no idea how not to. But it would be easier if I weren't surrounded by her entire life.

Somehow, I hadn't cried again today. But I could feel it building in my chest and knew it was coming. After Alex's shower, she only had a couple of hours to process what just happened before she left on tour again. I decided to give her the time.

"Oh." Stopped in the hallway between her bedroom and the bathroom, clad in a towel, she noticed me closing my suitcase on the couch. I met her gaze and sighed heavily. "Yeah."

She walked into her bedroom and came out in a tank and jean shorts. "I thought you could use some time by yourself before you leave again," I said to the floor.

She tilted my chin up so that I was looking right into her eyes, that blazing look back again. "I will love you always."

"Always. I wish I could make the world melt away."

"Me too."

I put my forehead against hers and we breathed together for a moment. Then, reluctantly, I broke our embrace and wheeled my case to the door and turned to her. She walked toward me and I cradled her face in my hands, memorizing every freckle and line. Tenderly, I sought her lips.

I thought everything I ever needed to know was in her kiss.

Perhaps it would be again someday.

We broke apart, and I held her hands in mine. In her eyes, I saw a hint of regret. I shook my head, silently telling her that this was the right thing.

I turned to the door, unlocked, and opened it, then stood facing her.

"Goodbye, Paige." She leaned against the door frame, backlit by the sunlight coming into the room, her golden hair lit up like a halo.

I bit my lip to keep from breaking down right there. "Goodbye, Alex."

FIFTEEN

Somehow, the worst break-ups I'd gone through were easier than this. I did not want to fall into the familiar pattern of heartbreak, then jealousy, then doing something a little dramatic. But that was the thing about my relationship with Alex. A part of me wasn't missing. She hadn't made me whole or completed me or any other Jerry Maguire-esque conclusion.

She complemented me. Alex saw me for who I truly was and I felt loved by her because when I was with her, I truly loved myself. I felt completely validated and accepted by her as my whole self: the oft-dramatic, sometimes-hard-shelled, impulsive, funny, complex person that I was. And that was significantly harder to let go of than any previous relationship. She was out there. She loved me.

But we couldn't be together.

And I saw the sense in it. I did. But I was already missing laughing with her so hard I cried. I was missing the curve of her neck. I was missing her cooking and her easygoing nature, the way she let things just roll off her back. I missed the woman who loved the Cubs and lived out loud and didn't care what anyone thought of her. I missed her joy and the little mole on her left hip. My heart didn't feel broken. It felt like it was constantly breaking.

After saying goodbye to Alex, I went back to my tiny studio apartment and collapsed on the bed. I had a perfunctory call with my dad during which I relayed the information, but I didn't stay on the line long. He told me he loved me and if I needed him, to call. It was nice to have that at the back of my mind. Dev and Kat had both sent supportive texts when I told them, but I didn't respond.

I spent Saturday night and Sunday ignoring my phone, watching mindless reality television, and crying intermittently. I needed to do that so that when Monday rolled around, I'd be ready to rehearse and forget about the wretched weekend I'd just had.

August turned to September the Monday after our break-up and, happily, I could throw myself into my work. And it was all ramping up. That week, we were going to see the set at the theater for the first time. I was doing another Instagram takeover of the show's account, so I would be spending Wednesday snapping pictures and stories of our process. The local television station was coming in to do an on-camera interview with me and some of the production crew. Toby and I were going to do a joint interview with a couple of the local newspapers as well as another with *Broadway World* and *Playbill.*

The online buzz around the show was building to a roar. There is nothing like a Broadway fan, and a new original musical was like a drug to them. In all honesty, I was enjoying being in the spotlight. Not only was it something I had worked so hard for, it was kind of nice to be fawned over, especially now that my heart was broken. Playing a lead in an almost-definitely-heading-to-Broadway show was a dream come true. And I was fairly certain they would ask me to stay on when it went to New York. They wouldn't be putting me out in front so much if they weren't.

Unless I was totally wrong and they were just being nice. My insecurities really wouldn't shut up sometimes.

I found the pain I was feeling at the loss of Alex could be set aside when I was working. Mostly, when I got home at night from rehearsal, when I posted on the show's Instagram, when I was on our union breaks, all I wanted to do was call her. Post about her. Hear her funny stories and have her listen to my frustrations. I knew from her social media that she was still on tour, and I was anticipating our reunion on opening night. I didn't think her mind would have changed, but if it did, I was more than ready to take her back. A tiny part of me still believed we could have made it work. Nothing was set in stone yet.

That Friday evening at the end of rehearsal, six full days after Alex and I had said goodbye, Andrea called the cast together and we all collapsed on the floor in front of her, sipping from water bottles and stretching.

"I want you to rest up this weekend. Because Monday we go into tech."

We all groaned, even though we knew it was coming. Tech week, or in our case, tech week and a half, is always kind of a nightmare. In a way, it's exciting. The show was about to come together with sets, lights, costumes, sound, but I knew it would be a slog to get there. Each cue would need to be worked out, blocking would need to be adjusted for the stage, we would have to adjust to the set, costume changes would need to be accounted for, and props would need to be put in all the right places.

The production was going to be a spectacle, and I couldn't wait to see it come together. But getting there was the hard part. So many moving pieces would be seamless in a few weeks, but for now, it was hard work. And I was grateful to have it. For most of the show, I was onstage, so while there would be some standing around, I knew a lot of my time was going to be taken up. I wouldn't be able to check my phone to see if she'd texted or to scroll her social media. I was going to fully immerse myself in this experience and try to keep Alex at the back of my mind.

Before she let us go, Andrea went through our schedule for Monday. We would arrive at the Cadillac Palace at ten in the morning and all go in together to see the set for the first time. This would be filmed for social media. And then the real work would begin.

"All right, team. I am so happy with the work you've done, and I can't wait to put everything together. You have made me, Toby, and everyone here so incredibly proud." Andrea was getting a little emotional. "When you workshop a musical, you never know where the original work is going to take you. And I can say that you have all been so flexible, so talented, and so wonderful to work with."

"Let's put on a show."

A cheer erupted from all of us. We were ready to get out of the rehearsal studio and onto the stage.

"Does it feel real?" Dev asked me as we followed our castmates to the elevator bank.

"Not yet. I feel like I'm dreaming so far."

"Me, too. But just imagine. Your kingdom is waiting for you."

I smiled at him, trying to share in his joy, and we piled into the elevator with our cast. We all burst out into the fading light of the early September evening.

"Holy shit, who is that?" I heard Steph say. We all looked over to the street corner. A figure stood leaning against a mailbox, his brown curls falling onto his forehead. "He is gorgeous."

The same hazel eyes as mine surveyed the crowd and landed on me.

"Sam!" I cried and hurried over to him, grinning. He hugged me tight and I felt tears sting the corners of my eyes.

"What are you doing here?" I said when I pulled back. Gratitude filled my heart. My big brother.

"I thought you could use the company. Surprise?" He looked unsure as to what my reaction would be. In response, I threw my arms around him again.

"Thank you," I said quietly. He squeezed a little harder. I turned away and said to my castmates. "This is my brother, Sam. He's visiting for the--" I turned to him, eyebrows raised. "-- weekend?"

Sam nodded.

Steph was practically drooling. He'd always had that effect on people.

I decided I wanted to have a little brother-sister time. "We're going for dinner. See you guys on Monday."

Everyone dispersed, but not before Dev came over to say hello to Sam, whom he had met on previous New York visits. "Stop it, you're salivating," I whispered to make him go away.

Dev dragged Steph and her bedroom eyes down the block. I chuckled.

"I can't believe you're here," I told Sam once we were alone.

"Dad said you sounded a little heartbroken on the phone. And you didn't answer my text about that old *Animaniacs* episode. So I knew something was up. I had the weekend free. Thought I'd visit my little sister."

We locked eyes and I grinned. "You love me."

"Shut up." He locked his arm around my neck and rubbed the top of my head with his knuckles. Playfully, I shoved him away. We took the train back to my neighborhood where we sat outside at my favorite bar. The sky was pink, the beers were cold, and my big brother was there to help heal my broken heart.

"So, what happened?" he said when our beers were set in front of us and we'd ordered some food.

Never any pretense with Sam. I chuckled. "Well, after the Broadway in Chicago concert--"

"I'm sorry we couldn't be there, but Jeff only gets married once. Probably." He rolled his eyes at the thought of our younger cousin.

"And of course he chose a Friday date." I rolled my eyes, too.

Sam sipped his beer. "But I would have loved to see you up there."

"I sent the video."

He shrugged. "Not the same."

A comfortable silence fell during which I felt so supported, and not just by Sam. I knew he was sent as an envoy for my dad and other brothers, too.

"Well, after the concert, we went out with the cast and had a great time. Alex was totally there for me, completely supportive, cried during my song. I was-- God, Sam, it was the best night of my life. Truly. I can't even put it into words.

"But when Alex and I got home, she immediately burst into these sobs. Like, just gut-wrenching, out-of-control sobs." I gave him a truncated version of the rest of the break-up, and the sweet goodbye that followed the next day. I left out the apron bit.

I swiped at my face with my napkin, getting rid of the few tears that had escaped as I told the story. I took a sip of beer and met his eyes. He was giving me a look I'd never seen before.

"You really loved her, huh?"

My throat caught, and I gazed upward at the darkening sky. "Love. I really do, yeah." I traced my thumb in the sweat on my beer glass, as cold as the feeling in my chest.

"But she's moving to L.A.?" His expression was mystified.

I nodded morosely. "Most likely."

"And that's the only reason she broke up with you?" I could see him trying to find the reasonable explanation, to get to the answer that I knew wasn't there.

"Not the only. Think about it, Sam. We are almost never going to be in the same place at the same time. I'm going to be doing eight shows a week--cross your fingers-- once I'm back in New York. Not to mention a month from now when we open. She's currently on tour. She'll be doing that all the time. In what world is that a relationship?"

"So what, your options are to date people who do theater professionally, or just not fall in love with anyone?" Sam was suddenly furious. "How is that fair?"

My eyebrows shot up. He wasn't usually this demonstrative. "That's not what I said."

"Sounds like it. People make it work, Paige. People put in the time and the effort. If it's worth it to you, you will make it work with someone. I'm not talking about you, personally, I'm talking about Alex. If she really loved you, she would have made the effort. She would have said 'screw L.A. and screw everything, you're the love of my life.'" He paused, his brow set and his mouth in an angry line. His expression changed suddenly, his lips turning up into a bemused grin. "I can't believe I want to punch a woman in the face so bad."

I knew he was joking and I gave him a wan smile. "I appreciate the sentiment, but please do not."

His eyes met mine. He was laughing a little. "I won't. I would never. Promise."

"Also, I don't need my big brother punching people for me. I took kickboxing classes for a reason."

He tipped his glass in my direction. "You always have been able to look after yourself."

I sniffled as another comfortable silence fell. Sam took a pull of his beer and our entrees arrived. For a few moments, we munched our food and then he met my eyes again. "I still think it's bullshit."

I sighed and put my fork down. "Sam. Regardless of what could have worked, how hard it would have been, or whatever--" My eyes filled again as I came to a realization. "Alex didn't *want* to. She didn't want... me." I felt a sob escape and I buried my face in my hands. I didn't want to see the look on Sam's face. And then I felt him next to me, wrapping an arm around my shoulders.

I leaned into him and let the tears come. I was trying to quell the loud sobbing, but I was definitely outright crying on the patio of this bar that I loved.

I could feel Sam take his wallet out and heard the server come over and take his card. Buried in Sam's shoulder, I heard someone else clear our plates.

"Bad break-up," Sam whispered over my head. I just kept crying, almost feeling good about still being my dramatic self. The server brought back Sam's card and to-go boxes with our barely touched meals in them. "Up you get, kiddo."

I wiped my face on the cloth napkin and stood shakily. He kept his arm around my shoulders as we maneuvered around the fence of the patio, and then we were on a tree-lined side street headed back to my place. I sniffled once more and wiped my eyes with the napkin again.

Sam tugged on the corner of the napkin. "You're a thief."

"Oh no. I stole their napkin." I could feel myself tearing up again.

"Don't cry about it. Just bring it back next time," Sam said, a note of exasperation and affection in his voice.

He was always there to pick me up like this. I had had no idea how much I needed my brother to help me through this.

Back at my studio, I calmed down significantly and spread our food on the coffee table. We flopped on the loveseat together.

"Feel better?" Sam asked before taking a huge bite of his burger.

"Much, actually. You would not believe how much I've cried lately. Did you miss me?" I was joking, but his response was real.

"I miss you all the time."

I paused in slicing up my salmon and looked at him. "Thanks for being here, Sam."

He gave me a closed mouth smile through another mouthful of burger, grease dripping down his chin. "You bet," he managed to get out. I genuinely laughed, put a forkful of salmon in my mouth, and reached for the remote.

We spent the weekend goofing around the city, though avoiding spots like Wrigley Field and a favorite pizza place because they would remind me of Alex. We watched movies from our childhood that had us laughing so hard tears streamed down our faces, and we reminisced about all the pranks we'd pulled on Tom and Josh when we were teenagers.

At the end of the weekend, I felt cleansed and closer to my brother than I had in years. At the front door to my building, we hugged tightly.

"Thanks for coming, Sam. I really needed this."

"I'll always be here for you. You can call me anytime."

We pulled away as his Lyft pulled up.

"Hey, if you see Alex at the opening, be nice, okay?" I called as he walked away.

He turned and gave me a grin. "No promises."

I chuckled. "Bye, Sam."

"Bye, Paige."

I watched his car pull down the street and turn left, then trudged back up to my apartment where I cleaned up the takeout boxes and folded the sheets and blankets he'd slept on the loveseat with. My heart, though it felt like a piece of it broke every day, seemed repaired in a small way. Sam had at least applied some stitches and bandages.

I could make it through this.

And tomorrow, I would see my castle.

SIXTEEN

I stood in front of the Cadillac Palace Theater with Dev and the rest of my cast. The air around us crackled and zinged with our excitement. Movement beyond the glass doors stilled us until they swung open dramatically. Andrea stepped out with a cameraman next to her, a professional rig strapped to his chest. She nodded toward me and he gave me a smile as he trained it on my face.

I grabbed Dev's hand and bounced a little on my toes. This was it.

"Come on in, folks," Andrea called.

Anticipation flowed through us and as a pack we walked through the front doors and into the ornate lobby of the theater. A sea of red carpet spread out in front of us, under gold and cream columns and balconies which were covered in filigrees. It already looked royal, and this was just the lobby. We traipsed through, our shoes whispering across the thick carpet, to the center door of the house.

The cameraman was in front of me walking backwards expertly, as though he'd done this a thousand times before, which he likely had.

Andrea gave me a secret smile. "Are you ready to see your palace, Paige?"

I nodded, exhilaration flowing through me, and she opened the door. We walked in at the back of the audience under the balconies. Spread out before us was a sea of empty red seats, and above and around them, the cream, gold, and green filigrees continued. It was opulence and decadence and extremely beautiful. We moved as one down the aisle.

The lights were brought up onstage and as we walked toward it, the grand red curtains opened, revealing our set.

My hand flew over my heart and I gasped. Dev clasped my other hand in his and let out a giggle of joy. A general sense of awe flowed through the air as we took in the magnificent view.

The forced perspective of the set showed us a medieval square in the center of a stone castle, which rose above the stage regally. A grand set of stairs painted silver and gold stood in the middle of it all, down which I would enter for the first time. Several layers of balconies, on which various scenes would play out, were richly painted to look like real stone. Opulent turrets on either side of the stage were functional, and I would be standing in one of them at several points in the show. At stage left was a wishing well that would actually function. A trap door underneath it would open and a crew member below the stage would fill the bucket with water.

A rumbling came from below the stage and the set began to move. On runners, the well was brought off stage left. At the same time on stage right, a bedroom set, Cassandra's quarters festooned with pink candelabras and purple fabric, arrived smoothly. As if by magic, the lighting dimmed on the bedroom set and it was brought off again. A starry night scrim, a transparent curtain, came down smoothly in the middle of the stage. It held a million twinkle lights, and in the inky, romantic darkness, I knew this is where I would sing "I Am Standing". My heart pounded. I was beaming, enchanted.

The magic continued: the scrim flew out and the castle rumbled away on the fly system. We could just barely hear the rush of the ropes and pulleys. A lush, green forest appeared: the place where Cassandra would meet Monet and her coven. The forest floor was made of what looked like real moss, so rich I felt I could lie down on it and sleep peacefully. The trees looked so real I wanted to climb them. On more runners, large boulders were moved in on stage right, and a small set of the inside of a cozy cottage appeared on stage left.

Again, the fly system changed it all back to the castle set and the wishing well came back. Suddenly, for what I knew would be the finale, banners unfurled from the turrets and walls. Two larger ones came down with a 'whoosh' from the fly lines all the way upstage. The banners, in a bold, dynamic yellow, bore the letter 'C'. The kingdom was Cassandra's.

Half of us were crying, I could hear the sniffles behind me. The camera was still trained on our faces. And I don't know if it was the fact that I'd cried so many tears already in the past week, or if I was just feeling strong enough, but I didn't. I simply felt at home.

I felt Cassandra and I merge. This was our kingdom. This was where I belonged.

After the set reveal, we were taken backstage and shown to our dressing rooms. This was the first time I would get my very own. For the first half of this first day in the theater, we would get acclimated to the space while the production crew set themselves up at their folding table, which would now be located in the theater itself about twenty rows back.

"Here you go, Paige." Our stage manager, Mel, with a huge grin on her face, opened the door with my name on it. I entered the room, closed the door behind me, and really took it in.

It wasn't glamorous, but it was all mine. About eight by ten feet, it had cinderblock walls and a big cushy chair in the corner. Next to that, a clothing rack held all of my costumes. Opposite it, a wooden chair sat in front of the white counterspace and a mirror with the requisite line of lightbulbs around it.

I set my bag on the floor and walked over to the costume rack. I ran my hand over the silks and the taffeta, then over my more badass Act Two costumes, mostly a combination of leather and lace. Turning, I caught a glance of myself in the mirror. My eyes were dancing. My heart was racing. I pulled out the chair and took a seat, placing my palms flat on the smooth surface in front of me. I stared directly into my own eyes, and it finally sunk in.

This was my dressing room. These were my costumes. That was my set. This was my place. I thought of every member of the cast and crew that I had collaborated with, who I valued so much, who had let me make mistakes and take the time to find Cassandra.

I was born for this. And I had finally made it. I bowed my head and thanked my lucky stars and everyone who had brought me here. When I looked back up at myself in the mirror, I felt stronger than I had ever been.

Turning away from the mirror, I started to unpack my bag when there was a knock on the door. "Come in."

"Am I allowed to consort with the star, or does she need her alone time in her chambers?"

"Get in here, Dev." I pulled him in by the hand and he surveyed the room.

He caught my eye and we smiled secretly at each other for a moment, then he wrapped his arms around me and squealed. I joined him and we hopped around joyfully.

When we'd finally calmed down, he caught my eye in the mirror. "So what do you think of your castle?"

I beamed at him. "It's perfect."

§

As predicted, tech was a slog, but the week still flew by. It was thrilling to see the show coming together, and to get to play on the set with some of my favorite people. It seemed like we were settling into our roles in a way that felt like putting on a comfortable sweater. I couldn't wait until we had an audience.

Alex had flitted in and out of my thoughts, an intermittent pain in my heart. I tried to put it aside most of the time, but at night, alone, it was impossible not to remember every perfect frame of our time together. Every day that I got closer to opening night, to seeing her, seemed to simultaneously give me hope and send me reeling with sadness.

"I have a surprise for you." Dev stood in my dressing room doorway, tossing an apple up and down like a cartoon villain.

Slinging my bag over my shoulder, I caught the apple and took a bite.

"Hey!" he said in mock consternation. I wiped apple juice off my chin and gave him a grin. "Brat. Come on, let's go. You're going to love this."

I skipped beside him. "I love presents."

"I know."

We went out the stage door. There, standing in the small parking area in front of the loading dock garage doors was Kat. I gaped for just a moment before running to her and body slamming her into a hug. We shrieked with delight and jumped around the parking lot.

"I love how many surprise guests I've been getting. This is the best!" I exclaimed.

Kat looked me right in the eyes. "I missed you, girl."

I squeezed her close then I pulled back and peered at her. "Wait, aren't you coming to the opening?"

"Of course I am. But I'm here now because you won't be able to do a lot of partying that weekend. And Dev and I made an executive decision that this weekend, you need to *party*."

I glanced over at Dev, who was munching on his apple. He gave me a devilish grin.

"You've done the wallowing. Let's do the irresponsible party-too-hard-out-til-dawn part of a breakup."

I grinned at her and over at Dev, gratitude flowing through my heart.

Kat took my hands and peered at me seriously. "Are you really okay?"

I sighed. "When I'm not thinking about it."

"Which is when?"

"Never."

"Oh, no. None of this maudlin shit, my girls." Dev tossed his apple core into a nearby trash can and stepped between us, threading his arms through ours. "Tonight is a night for bad decisions, questionable dance partners, and Lady Gaga. Rain on me, queens, let's go!"

Laughing boisterously, we marched to the train, led by Dev on a mission. We rode it up to Boystown, where we dumped our bags at Dev's and ordered Thai food. Over noodles, we joked and caught up with Kat, enjoying each other's company.

A couple of hours later, we all changed into skimpy clothes and layered on some makeup. I looked at Kat's reflection next to mine in the full-length mirror on the back of Dev's apartment door. "I have not looked like this since I was twenty-five." I pulled at the tight black tank dress Kat had given me out of her suitcase. She wore a pair of leopard print shorts and a black crop top with sky high heels.

"You look fuckin' sexy is what you look like. Come on, let's go make out with someone." Her voice dripped with delicious danger.

A recklessness overtook me then and I danced down the stairs after Kat and Dev. This was going to be the last big hurrah before the show took over my life more than it already had. When we started previews, I needed to be on my best behavior, saving my voice, protecting my body, and in general, being really lame.

So tonight, I was going to scream sing to Ariana Grande and grind up on whomever wanted me to, eat pizza at three in the morning, and drink to excess. Maybe by morning, I would have forgotten about Alex entirely.

Hah. Not a chance.

Dev led us to Roscoe's where a crush of mostly men scrambled around the bar to get noticed by the bartenders. Dev joined them with a wink at us. Kat and I yelled over the pump of the dance music, catching up on each other's lives. After fifteen minutes, Dev finally made his way back to us with three neon green drinks in plastic cups in one hand and three test tube shots in the other.

"Your fingers are in my drink, Dev," Kat admonished him.

He glared at her but there was a twinkle in his eye. "Your hero returns with alcohol and you get mad at him for managing to get it here safely? Shut up and drink."

We each took a test tube and a cup. Dev raised his test tube. "To not having any idea that this moment happened at the end of tonight," he yelled.

I caught Kat's eye and saw mischief there. This was exactly what I needed.

"To not remembering anything!" I called.

"To drinking to forget, a completely healthy pastime!" Kat said.

All three of us downed our test tube shots then made our way to the back of the bar to a dark, exposed brick-walled room where a DJ was blasting a Madonna dance remix. We began to move, drinking the neon green drinks faster than I thought we would. I couldn't hear a thing, just felt the crush of bodies and the music pumping through my chest. I closed my eyes and raised my hands above my head, feeling free of the pain of the past few weeks.

That, of course, caused Alex's perfect face to swim across my mind. I motioned to Kat and Dev that I was going to get more drinks. They waved me away. I made my way to the bar in the back as Miley Cyrus' new single pulsed through me.

Someone danced into me as I tried to get in line causing me to bump into the person in front of me. "Sorry, sorry!" I yelled, hoping they could hear and trying to straighten myself up.

"Hey, no problem."

My gaze locked onto the goddess I'd run into. She was taller than me with messy blonde hair that looked like it had been slept on. Her bright blue eyes took me in with a full up and down tilt of her head. When her eyes met mine, after they were done skimming my whole body, they were swimming with desire. An entire sleeve of tattoos decorated her arm and without thinking, since I was two drinks in, I reached out and stroked a colorful flower.

"Is that a peony?" I stretched up so I could yell in her ear.

She ignored my question. "You're really cute."

Suddenly shy, I just smiled and licked my lips slowly, stroking another colorful tattoo. Was I hitting on her?

She watched my hand trail down her arm. "Are you hitting on me?"

"Do you want me to?" Where was this coming from? I glanced back over at Dev and Kat as the goddess turned and leaned over to the bartender, shouting her drink order in his ear. They both gave me a geeky thumbs up.

The glamazon was back in front of my face. "Kinda." She raised an eyebrow, a devious smile playing across her lips. She had a drink in each hand and stepped close to me so that our hips met. She pressed herself closer, her breasts soft against me, and I felt a swooping of desire in my stomach. In my ear, she yelled, "Catch me on the dance floor."

She walked away and I watched her perfect ass until I couldn't see it anymore. I guess this really was going to be the night of bad decisions. I ordered three more neon green things--they were disgusting but cheap--and another test tube shot. I downed the shot then made my way back to Kat and Dev.

We drank more neon green drinks and lost ourselves to the music, the mess of bodies, the glistening sweat of other people, the pumping of the bass. At one point, I felt a hand around my waist. It was the glamazon. I turned to her and ground my hips into hers. As we danced in the middle of the floor, the red and yellow and blue and green lights flashed around us. I couldn't feel anything but her body against mine. Some time ago, I had set my drink down, leaving my hands free to roam over her arms and waist.

She was tall and packed with muscle, incredibly sexy. Alex's softness ran through my mind, her sweet smile and gentle touch. I shook my head, clearing the vision and turned my back to the glamazon. She held my hips and we thrummed as the music coursed through our bodies. I raised my arms up behind me and put them around her neck. My back arched, my ass thrust into her thighs. She snuck one arm around my waist, placed her other hand on my chin and turned my face to hers. I licked my lips in anticipation and her lips met mine, insistent and prying, her tongue darting around mine. There was no softness to her lips, not like the tenderness I was used to with Alex, even when we were furious and passionate.

It felt completely wrong.

This wasn't my Alex. This woman, who I thought was beautiful and was probably very smart and fun, her lips weren't right on mine. They didn't fit. I pulled away and gave her a wan smile before grabbing Dev and Kat's hands and dragging them through the swarm of dancers and out of the bar. We spilled onto the sidewalk, the sudden quiet shaking our equilibrium.

"Well, first make-out post break-up. How do you feel?" Kat said.

I stood, staring out at the street, watching people getting on with their lives. My arms were crossed in front of me and I felt a little numb, plus a little wobbly from the four drinks I'd already consumed. And then it hit me like a lightning bolt, what I had tried to ignore for the entire evening. I groaned and doubled over.

"I miss Alex."

Out of the corner of my eye, I saw Kat and Dev share an alarmed look.

"Oh no, let's go!" Dev practically dragged me to Sidetrack across the street where we danced along to the "Time Warp" from *The Rocky Horror Picture Show*. Then we somehow managed to get into Scarlet where Dev made eyes at all the gorgeous people and Kat watched him appreciatively. As we sipped yet another cocktail, Kat and Dev started getting handsy with each other. When I was at the bar to get us another--unnecessary bordering on destructive--round, I turned to find them making out. I rolled my eyes and marched back over to them.

"Oh hell no, you two, we are going home." They protested as I pulled them out of the bar.

Reluctantly, they followed me as we stumbled down the block. We found a place to buy a giant slice of pizza and shared it on our way back to Dev's where eventually all three of us draped ourselves across his furniture and passed out.

§

"Dev..." I heard Kat moan in the possibly-morning-but-likely- afternoon.

"Kat. Shut. Up." Dev's muffled reply came from somewhere on the floor.

"Did we kiss?"

I opened one eye and brushed my hair off my forehead.

Dev bolted up from the floor where he was covered in all of Kat's clothes. Her open suitcase sat nearby, empty. I briefly remembered deciding we were going to dress him up. When he'd passed out on the floor, we'd covered him in the clothes instead, giggling like schoolgirls.

"We didn't," he said, suddenly alert. He plucked a shimmery tank top off of his shoulder.

"You did," I told them, scrubbing my hand down my face.

They both groaned.

I chuckled from Dev's armchair. I was at an impossible angle, one leg slung over one arm with my back against the other. I groaned and put both feet on the floor.

"Let us never speak of it," Kat mumbled from her position, face down on the couch.

"Never," Dev agreed, and fell back onto the clothes again.

I snickered again and cast about for my phone. I found it wedged between my hip and the back of the chair. An email from the production manager. I opened it.

> Hello, *On Her Own* Cast Members,
>
> The show is really shaping up and I am getting very excited for previews. I am reminding you that each cast member is allotted two tickets to opening night, though they are not guaranteed to sit together. Please fill out the attached form with the names of the attendees you would like to claim your comps.
>
> Thank you, and break legs in dress next week!

I opened the Google form and typed in my dad's name. I paused as I remembered the glamazon from last night and how wrong her lips felt against mine. Then I remembered a different pair of soft lips, the rush of creamy skin, laughter in the early morning.

I typed in *Alexandra Tate*.

SEVENTEEN

The rest of the weekend was spent downing water and eating healthy foods, moaning with Dev and Kat. It was a stark reminder of why we didn't go out like that anymore. Thirty was hitting hard and my voice was protesting, too. I spoke as little as possible to rest my vocal chords while I kept flashing back to the moment on Roscoe's dance floor. I realized that it wasn't just being in a relationship or consensual groping that I wanted. I didn't want to be desired by just anyone.

I only wanted Alex.

And that was not going to happen.

I needed to buck up and move on. My hope about seeing her face on opening night changed. Instead of hoping we could work it out, I wanted it to provide some kind of closure to our relationship.

When I'd texted her that her ticket would be at the box office, she'd sent back a heart emoji. I didn't know how to take that so I didn't respond. Then she'd texted: *Can't wait.*

My fingers had hovered over the keyboard, but I couldn't think of what to say. So I left it and didn't hear anything else from her.

Kat left Sunday evening with promises that she would return for opening night, and I spent the rest of the night in my apartment going over the script and my music, prepping for the last few tech rehearsals. Honeyed tea seemed to help a slight scratchiness I felt in my throat. That was good, because by the end of the week, we would be running with full costumes and tech: dress rehearsals. I tried to get excited, but my dulled senses were not cooperating.

Our first previews, when audiences would be allowed in, were only a week away. While those ran, we would be tweaking the parts of the show they didn't respond to, making the final touches. I was anxious to begin getting feedback.

In my dressing room the night of the first dress, I sipped Throat Coat tea to soothe my voice. I prepped my hair and makeup then stripped down to my underwear. After strapping my mic pack around my waist, I pulled the wire up, and threaded it through my hair. With that pinned in place, I stepped into my first costume and turned to look at myself in the mirror.

Cassandra stared back at me, all at once innocent and fierce. "Let's go on this journey, queen," I told her. I exited my dressing room and heard places being called. A frisson of excitement ran through the hallway from the cast and crew and settled down deep into my chest. Finally, I could feel it.

I knew I'd get there.

We knew this show by now, backwards and forward. And sure, there might be changes. Feedback would be taken under advisement and there was a chance that songs could get moved or entire scenes cut. But I felt like we had a really good show.

"Paige."

I turned.

Toby looked me over, ready to play the character he envisioned. His expression softened and it looked like he was going to cry. "You incredible woman. Break a leg tonight." He took my hands in his and squeezed.

"I hope I make you proud."

He kissed me on the cheek. "You already do."

The orchestra started the overture. I cleared my throat and went upstairs to take my place behind the proscenium for my entrance. I closed my eyes...

...And felt like when I opened them again, it was a week later and I stood in the same place. Previews were about to begin and I didn't feel as confident as I had the week before. I cleared my throat as I stood at the ready, long before places were called, the nerves beginning to get to me. I shook my hands out and paced around the bottom of the utilitarian wooden staircase that would take me up to the entrance of the grand one onstage. The curtain was already open to the audience and I could hear the murmur of theatergoers riffling through Playbills, taking their seats, sipping their wine. I breathed deeply when I heard our stage manager call "Places!"

I reminded myself that I was Cassandra.

But just before I shook my own self off and stepped into her skin, I wished desperately that I could speak to Alex. There wasn't some ban on talking to each other, we'd just seemed to come to a tacit understanding that it was easier not to communicate. I had reached for my phone a dozen times in the last two weeks, wanting to talk out some frustration or another, but really just to hear her bell-like laugh. Her husky voice. To tell her how much she meant to me. I knew it was for the best, even if it consumed me every night before I fell asleep.

The last section of the opening number reached my ears and I banished all thoughts of Alex, rolling my shoulders.

I closed my eyes.

I climbed the stairs.

I made my entrance.

§

Thunderous applause every night that first weekend of previews was giving all of us a lot of confidence as we zoomed toward opening night. We knew Toby was working on a few changes before he froze the show, but our audiences had laughed and clapped enthusiastically every night. If previews were any indication, *On Her Own* was going to Broadway. I fell asleep on Sunday night feeling proud and satisfied.

But on Monday morning, someone was coughing, and when I opened my eyes, I realized it was me. I had woken myself up with a deep, hacking cough that instantly set my nerves on edge. I reached for the water bottle on my bedside table and took several long gulps. Sitting stock still, I waited for another fit of coughing to come on, but it seemed to have passed.

Then I realized what this meant.

Very, very quietly, almost at a whisper, I hummed and trilled my lips for several minutes. A tiny bit louder, I tried to vocalize through an arpeggio.

It hurt. Minimally, but it was not smooth, and not just because it was the morning. My eyes filled with tears and I willed them away, knowing they would only make this worse. With a shaking hand, I reached for my phone in the half-darkness, my mind nearly blank as I feared the worst. I pressed icons until I heard ringing.

"Paige, what's happened?" mumbled a sleepy voice.

"Toby, I--" I cut myself off with a gasp when I heard the hoarseness in my voice.

"No." His voice was firm and I could tell he'd sat up in an instant.

"I don't know what to--"

"*Don't speak*. Do not talk. Make yourself a tea but don't drink it until it's lukewarm. I'll call you back in a few."

I nodded and didn't mind that he hung up on me. Tears were threatening again and I raised my eyes to the ceiling, willing them away. I would not cry. I could not cry. Slowly, I got out of bed and turned on my kettle. I pulled out a bag of Throat Coat and placed it in a mug, staring at the water boiling as I silently cursed myself for pushing too much.

The weekend out with Dev and Kat. All the crying over Alex. And before that, a summer of cheering at the roller derby and the Cubs game, Pride, all of the alcohol. I had not been kind to my voice, my instrument, my livelihood, and without it, everything good in my life was going to disappear. I tried to keep the panic at bay, but my hands shook as I poured the boiling water.

I set the mug down on my bedside table and sank back into my pillows. This couldn't be what I thought it was. I could not deal with this on top of everything else. As I waited for the tea to cool and Toby to call me back, I experimentally--and probably unwisely--tried an arpeggio again.

Bad.

Oh god.

I had nodes.

Vocal fold nodules. A singer's worst nightmare. Little callouses that form on your chords if you don't take care of your voice or if you sing incorrectly for too long. I could swear I was taking care of myself, despite some bad decisions. I worked with our vocal coach every day to make sure everything I was singing was technically perfect in order to avoid *this exact thing*.

I almost groaned aloud until I realized that Toby would have my head. My phone rang. Think of the devil.

"Do not talk. I just spoke with Mel and she's put in a call to our local otolaryngologist."

Leave it to Toby to pronounce that word correctly at five in the morning.

"We don't know when he is available. But until further notice, you are on vocal rest, do you understand me? Vocal. Rest. Do not talk, hum, sing, or do anything with your voice. Tea and a steam if you have it. Lots of water, and don't eat anything that might upset your stomach."

I nodded when he paused, even though he couldn't see me.

"And don't get upset, but we are going to have to have a put- in rehearsal tomorrow morning, a companywide email is going out soon. Just in case Tasha has to step in tomorrow night."

I closed my eyes. My understudy, Tasha, was truly incredible, but I couldn't believe I might have to give up Cassandra this soon, especially since it meant such upheaval with the company. If we needed Tasha to cover my track, then the rest of the cast would have to cover hers. As my swing, she had the least to do in the ensemble, but still. I was screwing this up for everyone.

"You are my Cassandra, Paige. Always, forever." He'd read my mind. "And I'm sure this is nothing. But if it is..." He sighed heavily, barely wanting to say the words. "If it is nodes, we will deal with it."

My eyes filled again at the comfort he brought me.

"And no *crying*," he growled before he hung up on me again. I laughed silently then turned on the shower to steam up the bathroom and stayed there for a long, long time.

Later, bundled up in my coziest robe, I sipped more tea and checked my phone. A text from Mel, my stage manager.

> Paige, so sorry to hear about your voice. We're going to do everything we can to help. I have made an appointment for you with Dr. Jefferson James. He's the best in the city and the only one we trust. It's on Thursday morning at ten as unfortunately he's out of town until then.
>
> We will have to put Tasha in for the Tuesday, Wednesday, and Thursday shows, just to be safe. Put-in is tomorrow morning at 11. We have a few changes to go over as well, and I don't want you to miss anything. I know this is hard, but we'll get you back in shape! Until then, vocal rest. See you tomorrow.

I sighed. Three days without talking, three days without performing, and three days to ruminate on whether or not my career was over.

Fantastic.

EIGHTEEN

At eleven on the nose the next day, I strolled onto the stage, a giant water bottle in my hand and a smile on my face. Whatever else happened, I led this company, and I was not about to let them down by showing how terrified I was.

"There she is," Dev said as he sidled up to me. He wrapped me in a life-threatening squeeze. He'd been sending me encouraging texts for the past twenty-four hours and I returned his affection, pleased to have him on my side.

"You're going to be fine," he whispered. I squeezed a little tighter. He pulled back, his hands on my waist as he looked very seriously into my eyes. "You're going to be fine."

I tried to give him a small smile, then greeted my other cast members silently, accepting hugs and sympathetic pats on my shoulder. We all turned when Andrea cleared her throat from where she stood downstage.

"Well, we've had a bit of a hiccup. Paige is going to be on vocal rest until we can get her to the doctor, and therefore, Tasha is going to be taking over the role of Cassandra for the next four performances."

A jolt of jealousy ran through me but I caught Tasha's eye and smiled encouragingly. Her eyebrows were knitted together as she tried to smile back. I didn't want her to go into this filled with anxiety, so I walked over, slung my arm around her shoulders, and turned back to Andrea.

She smiled at us both. "As you all know, our swings are pretty much the most important people we've got. Tasha has been covering Cassandra's track but has only performed it once."

I had skipped the rehearsal at which Tasha went in to make sure she was prepared for something exactly like this. My intention had been to perform every show, and I hadn't wanted to make her feel uncomfortable by being there.

"We're going to run through the show as if it were a performance, but we may need to stop and start in certain places. And to add another complication, Toby is working on a few minor changes, so we'll be sending those on and adding them into tomorrow's shows. The matinee might feel a bit rough, but let's give it our all. For now, Tasha needs to feel your support. And so does Paige. Let's give them a hand."

That night, I leaned against the wall on stage left after confirming with the crew that I wouldn't be in anyone's way. As I watched Tasha move effortlessly around the stage in her Cassandra costumes, singing my songs, I tried to tamp down the rage I felt at myself for not taking better care. I couldn't cry, I couldn't scream my rage at Dev, I couldn't do anything at all but watch helplessly as Tasha performed.

My penchant for jealousy was one of the things I most hated about myself. And I was feeling it in spades. Tasha was incredible. She might have been better than me. I could see that I was easily replaceable, that if I had nodes and my career was over, I would not be missed.

I went home during the standing ovation. Back in my tiny box of a room, I paced back and forth, waiting for water to boil, feeling caged. I turned the shower on again, made my tea, and stepped into the steam. All of the things I had been trying not to feel seemed to surface and I felt the deepest despair I had ever known.

I slumped in the tub, my back against the cool porcelain. The steam whorled around me and I tried to breathe deeply. I had to keep myself from crying as everything seemed to surface. Tasha's perfect performance. The looks of pity on my castmates faces. That I couldn't call and talk to anyone, couldn't rage, couldn't cry. All I could do was bottle all of it up and shove it down, because if I thought too hard about it, I would start sobbing and never stop.

My career could be over. Nodules could require surgery. Surgery I might never recover from, and even if I did, my voice might never be the same. My whole life had led up to this moment and it might all come crashing down.

With a heavy heart, I crawled into bed, the horror of losing my voice plaguing every one of my dreams.

The changes from Toby came in the next morning: a couple of rearranged songs, a dropped scene that was really just filler, a few revisions to the script. Nothing I couldn't handle when I got back onstage. If I got back onstage. Sitting next to Andrea in the audience, I watched a run-through without tech or costumes. The changes made the show even better, and I couldn't help but think we had a genuine hit on our hands.

I hoped I'd get to be a part of it.

The cast gathered onstage before Andrea let them rest before the matinee and we made our way up to them. Something had changed in them. The air was charged with tension and they all had their phones out while looking shiftily around, whispering among themselves. More than one of them caught my eye and looked quickly away. Tasha's eyes were the size of saucers and her mouth hung open when she looked up from her phone. She caught my eye and shook her head.

Unable to speak, I stamped my foot. Loudly. It echoed around the stage like a gunshot and everyone stilled and looked over at us.

Andrea put a hand on my arm. "Explain yourselves," she demanded.

Dev was the one who stepped forward. I crossed my arms and glared at him.

"Check your phone. I sent the link. I don't think you should look at it, but that's your decision."

I pulled my phone out of my back pocket and opened my text thread with Dev. The link was to a Broadway gossip blog, run by a total ass of a man named Roger. I tried not to groan aloud as I clicked it.

**OMGCELEB EXCLUSIVE:
PAIGE PARKER KICKED OUT OF
PRE- BROADWAY PRODUCTION OF
*ON HER OWN***

We've got some good gossip for you today, kittens. Last night, for unknown reasons, Tasha Bedford was on the stage of the Cadillac Palace Theater in Chicago. The production of *On Her Own*, which has been workshopping and rehearsing for months in the Second City, was previously headed up by Paige Parker in her first starring role.

This is Parker's second Broadway (they're all hoping) production. Jury's out on whether or not she's talented, or whether she did something else to get the role. Who's to say? One can only speculate about her character. But do you remember how she behaved to our collective boyfriend, Ethan Carter, all those years ago?

Perhaps they got sick of all of Parker's drama. Perhaps she did something egregious and they had to let her go. Perhaps they realized she doesn't have the chops for a starring role on Broadway after all. Either way, the gorgeous Tasha Bedford is rumored to have brought the house down last night. And Parker was nowhere to be seen. We'll see what happens, but our bets are that she comes back here to New York, tail between her legs, begging for scraps.

I read through what Roger's twisted mind had come up with as Andrea read over my shoulder. I shuddered.

Most of the cast began talking at once. I heard snippets of *we'll Tweet about it* and *we'll tell Roger what's up, the menace* but they just washed over me. I stood stock still, full of rage, jealousy, and every ugly emotion I had been trying to keep myself from feeling.

Andrea silenced them all with a raised hand. "We'll issue a press release. Presumably, this came to our attention from our friends back in New York?"

"I got it from Dion Hart. He got it from someone else." Steph looked guilty as she said this. "So yeah, it's making the rounds."

I cast my glance down at the scuffed floor of the stage, suddenly unable to be around any of this any longer. Knowing that, like Roger the Menace said, I might be going back to New York, career in tatters, unable to sing, all of the hard work I put in, meaningless. All of my dreams that were so close, gone forever. Without acknowledging any of them, I turned on my heel and walked off of the stage and out of the theater.

Lying in bed that night, my mind was racing. I had received dozens of supportive texts from Toby, Dev, most of the cast, and even Andrea who almost never texted. Tasha had sent me a long email saying that she was honored to be trusted with the role I had created and took a lot of inspiration from me. While I was bolstered by the encouragement, it didn't change the fact that I was going to the doctor in the morning and he would confirm whether or not my career was over.

What would I do? Bartend again? Go back to school? Get the dangerous surgery with no guarantee that my voice would ever be the same? Teach dance? I had no idea what my life would look like if I had to leave the career I had worked so hard for. I tossed and turned, my throat tight, and I tried. I tried so hard not to, but I couldn't escape the tears. I succumbed to the sadness and uncertainty and let them come.

I rolled over onto my side and let the hot tears slide over my nose. I didn't make a single sound, but felt my pillowcase grow wet underneath my cheek. I desperately wished I had something to hold onto, and for the first time since I'd woken up coughing, Alex's face swam to the forefront of my mind. How I wished she were here. How I wished I could feel her steady heartbeat as she wrapped her arms around me from behind. How I wished I could hear her whisper words of comfort in my ear, promising me that everything would be okay.

The tears came hotter until I finally felt myself drift off, dreaming of Alex's arms around me.

In the morning, I had an email from our production manager with an attached press release. It cited that I had been taken out of the show for health reasons and the hope was that I would be returning as soon as I was able. The blog post had been removed.

Good. Suck it, Roger. You dick.

"All right, Ms. Parker. Let's see what's going on with your throat, shall we?" Dr. James had kind eyes and a bass quality to his voice that was incredibly comforting.

I nodded at him, my eyes surely betraying my fear. My hands were shaking. My mind was racing. The rest of my life would be determined in the next moments.

"I know you've been on vocal rest, and that's good." Dr. James put his warm hands on the side of my neck, pressing around my ears and down my throat with his thumbs. "I don't feel any swelling. That's a good sign."

I nodded again, my eyes wide.

Dr. James sat on a small stool and wheeled it closer to the exam table where I sat. His expression was full of sympathy. "Ms. Parker, I understand the gravity of what we're talking about here. I deal with singers all the time, and that includes my wife. I have a personal understanding of what you're going through. So rest assured, there are various options when it comes to vocal fold nodules. Please do not think that your career is over and that you'll never sing again."

I huffed slightly through my nose at that but gave him a small grin.

He gave me a genuine smile. "I know you're scared. But whatever we find today, we will chart a course of treatment, and go from there."

He then asked me a series of what felt like three hundred questions about my vocal health: how often did I sing before warming up, did I drink a lot, did I have a history of acid reflux... It felt like an eternity before he stood and wheeled the large monitor over and removed a metal gun-looking thing. I eyed the instrument warily.

"Now, we're going to take a look at your vocal folds. This will allow me to see what's going on down there. I'm going to insert this--" He indicated the long, flexible, rubber end of the metal gun thing. "--down your throat. It may be uncomfortable for a few minutes. Then I'm going to ask you to vocalize a bit, a hum will do, so we can see what we're working with. Does that sound okay?"

I nodded again. My heart seemed to want to thrum out of my chest. It was beating as fast as a hummingbird's wings. This was it.

"Okay, sit forward just a bit and open your mouth."

After the procedure, I sat on the table shaking, and sipping from a tiny cup of water. Dr. James was studying the monitor with a frown, twisting buttons and peering closer. I couldn't see it, so I had no idea what was happening, and the look on his face didn't indicate anything good. The anxiety twisted around my chest and I was starting to lose all hope. The nodes had to be worse than I thought.

My career was over. I closed my eyes, willing the weeping to wait until I had some privacy.

"Well, Ms. Parker, I apologize for the time that took, but I didn't want to give you false hope. The stroboscope has shown no nodules on your vocal folds. In fact, they look completely healthy. Vocal rest was the right choice."

My eyes were still closed as I let these words sink in, which took a few moments. I snapped them open to look at him.

"No nodes?" I whispered, my first words in days.

"None. It could have been allergies, or lack of sleep, or any number of things that made you feel sore and cough. But you've got a great instrument there, Ms. Parker. Use it wisely. I look forward to seeing the show."

Before I could stop myself, I threw my arms around him. I could hear his surprised chuckle as he kindly patted my back. I let go of him and stepped back, a bit embarrassed, feeling tears of happiness fill my eyes. "I'm sorry," I whispered. "I--"

He put a hand up to stop me, an amused grin spreading across his face. "I completely understand. Like I said, my wife is a singer."

I swiped at the tears running down my cheeks and whispered again, "Thank you."

"You're very welcome. Now, onward. Before you start speaking and singing normally again, I want you to go take a voice lesson and ease yourself back in to vocalizing. Drink lots of water, avoid dairy completely, and drink as little caffeine as you can stand. If you do that today, I think you could be back onstage tomorrow, as long as you get the okay from your voice coach."

I nodded. Once I'd conveyed my gratitude and left the office, I sent a companywide email with the results. Our voice coach reached out and scheduled a session with me immediately. Elated texts and emails came in from everyone, and Tasha sent the sweetest one thanking me for handing her the reins and giving her one more night to be Cassandra.

The voice lesson went perfectly. I breathed, hummed, trilled, and went through every scale as my voice felt warmer and warmer. After a while, I could sing through "I Am Standing" with ease once again. I couldn't keep the smile off of my face and neither could my coach. She confirmed that as long as she warmed me up before the next few performances, I could go on tomorrow.

Tomorrow.

I love ya, tomorrow.

NINETEEN

The last weekend of previews went perfectly. After the scare I'd had, I was more grateful than ever for the *On Her Own* company, these beautiful people who supported me and believed in me enough that I could be the star of this production. Back in Cassandra's mind, I floated through the show and we received a standing ovation each night.

They liked us. They really liked us.

I took it easy that last weekend and through the double show day on Wednesday. I performed. I ate. I slept. That's all it felt like I was doing. Eat. Perform. Sleep. Rinse, repeat. I was quite confident that opening night would be a smash.

But the day before, with the whole day off so we could rest and gear up for our big night, my nerves began to fray. Not because of the show, that was solidified in my bones.

But Alex would be out there.

I was probably the only one not grateful to have the time to think. I spent the morning lying in bed, twirling my phone in my hands, playing our movie montage relationship over and over in my mind. Reliving how I'd felt the night before my doctor appointment, when I felt the lowest I ever had, when I'd craved her arms around me. Finally, I caved.

"Paige?" Alex didn't sound surprised to hear from me.

"Hi."

"Hi."

A heavy silence followed. Hearing two words from her sent my heart reeling and I didn't know what to say next.

"What's up?" she asked gently.

"Tomorrow is opening." I wished I had a phone cord to twirl around my fingers like when I was a kid.

"I know. I'm really excited to see it."

"Do you think... Could you meet me for lunch? Or coffee? Or anything? Are you already in town?"

Another pause, this one loaded. "Yeah. The tour got extended but I've been home for a couple of weeks."

"Oh." A deep cut knifed across my abdomen. She'd been so near me and hadn't reached out. Not that I expected her to, but the reality of the break-up was too much. My eyes fluttered closed as I tried to think of what to say next.

She rescued me. "And I'm hungry. Mortar & Pestle?"

I relaxed a tiny bit. "Twenty minutes?"

"See you then."

We arrived at the same time and stopped in front of the door just short of touching each other. I gazed into her eyes and every memory that I'd replayed that morning, the ones I'd tried to shove away as I worked, came flooding to the front of my mind again. Simultaneously, we stepped together and wrapped our arms around each other.

I breathed in the scent of her, the familiar shampoo, and the sweetness that was unique to her. My heart was hammering in my chest and I was sure she could feel it. The golden thread between us throbbed, frayed but not yet broken. Her arms squeezed tighter around me and I felt her take a deep breath. Relief broke through me as I realized I wasn't the only one feeling regret.

We broke apart without speaking. Inside, we were seated immediately at the table where we'd had our first date. Feeling awkward, I met her eyes for a few moments. Both of us were clearly unsure what to do. Alex cleared her throat.

"I didn't really think about our first... you know, when I suggested it," she said sheepishly.

A small smile tugged at the corners of my mouth. "It's really good food. Don't worry about it."

We ordered coffees--decaf for me--and omelets, and then an awkward silence fell. I cleared my throat. This was my idea. I had to tell her why she was here, even though I couldn't quite articulate it myself. "I think that I needed to see you before you come tomorrow night. I wanted to be able to concentrate without wondering what the first words we would say to each other would be. Thank you for meeting me."

"I'm glad you called. It's good to see you." Across the table, Alex met my gaze with a look so despondent I wanted to move over and take her in my arms and kiss every pain away.

I sighed. In the ensuing silence, I could feel a million things going unsaid between us. I decided that if I was going to live the truth of Cassandra onstage, I might as well live my truth here and now. I inhaled deeply. "I miss you so much, Alex. I had a scare last week and I just wanted you to be there, to be with me." I waved away the alarmed look on her face. "It ended up being nothing, a vocal scare. But it felt like everything was ending, and I wanted you next to me. I can't stand not being with you."

A dam broke in her eyes. A heavy sigh escaped her, and it seemed filled with relief. "I have been so miserable without you. I hated coming home to an empty place. I wanted so badly to call you, but I didn't want to distract you while you prepared for opening. I mean, this is the biggest moment of your life. And I didn't want to emotionally sabotage you."

I snickered. "No, I decided to do that myself."

She chuckled and reached across the table as if on autopilot to take my hand. She stopped just before she touched my fingers, giving me a look of mild alarm. I took her hand in mine and squeezed. An entirely different look overcame her features. She looked ravaged. Guilty.

"I hate that I hurt you so badly." Her husky voice was barely above a whisper.

A familiar catch ran up my throat. "Is L.A. still a go?"

She nodded. "There's some contract stuff they're working out. But once that hurdle is cleared, I'll have to find a place." She pulled her hand back and rubbed her brow.

I spoke into my coffee, unable to meet her gaze. "Then you did the right thing. I hate it, don't get me wrong. It's stupid that we're not together. But I do understand."

"I wish I could change it."

I raised my shoulders and pressed my lips into what I hoped was a convincing smile. "But it's your career. And it's exciting."

Everything she'd been feeling seemed to come out in a whooshing breath. "It's bittersweet. I want to feel happy about it, and somewhere inside me, I am. But I can't find it. Not when I can't share it with you."

Her melancholy brown eyes met mine, and a heavy silence fell as we gazed at each other. Finally, I said, "I feel the same way. I should be every single anticipatory emotion right now: nervous, excited, scared. But I'm having a hard time finding the joy in what's about to happen to me, too."

Her eyebrows knit together and she looked as though I'd punched her. "Paige, I hate that you feel that way. This should have been the best time of your life, and I... I took that from you. I stole that joy. I can't--"

We were interrupted by our food being brought to us. I shook my head and looked out of the window, trying to keep back the tears that were threatening to fall. She thanked the server but we didn't pick up our forks.

I took a deep breath and turned back to her. "Alex, I wouldn't change those months with you for a moment. Every second with you was worth it."

She nodded, but I could still see the guilt in her eyes. After a moment's hesitation, she said, "I know I did the right thing. We can't have a cross country relationship. It would be impossible. You wouldn't even be able to come to L.A. very often. Not until you left the show--"

"I can take time off whenever. And I might not even be invited to the Broadway run." I wasn't sure why I was trying to make the case for us. I didn't want a relationship with her unless it could be everything.

Her expression turned incredulous. "If they don't ask you to play Cassandra on Broadway, they are blind and deaf and dumb. When you sang at the concert, you were magnificent."

I gazed at her, unable to form words. I tried to swallow over the catch in my throat. Hearing her say that was exactly what I needed before tomorrow night. My chest constricted and I willed myself not to cry in another restaurant. It was the last thing my voice needed.

"And the other thing is, we'll both move on eventually. There's eight billion people on this planet. And you're a catch. You're damn near perfect. I'm sure you'll be snapped up by someone immediately." There was a hint of jealousy in her voice. She played with the sugar spoon in her coffee, while averting her gaze from mine.

I stared at her, my breath coming faster and the hitch in my throat getting worse. If I told her everything I was feeling, she would have walked out of the restaurant. The last few weeks had made me realize something significant, something I couldn't stop thinking about.

I wanted to spend the rest of my life with her.

I could see it all: me and Alex and Sammy and maybe a dog and a little apartment and fulfilling careers and coming home together when we could. It was all laid out in front of me.

If things had been different.

"I don't want anyone else." My words came out stilted. It was all I could manage to say. My heart shattered hopelessly as I saw her face harden, a resolve straighten her shoulders.

"Not right now. But you will. And I will, too. And maybe someday we can be friends. But right now, this radio silence we've been doing, it's probably for the best. I can't wait to see you tomorrow night, and I'm really happy you invited me to the reception after, but..."

A flare of jealous anger rose up inside me at the thought of her finding someone else. But even through that, I could see she was struggling as she toyed with her fork. Finally, she looked me directly in the eyes.

"I think after tomorrow, maybe we should go back to the radio silence. I don't think I can handle communicating with you. Not until we get some more distance." Her voice was low and sad. She rubbed a hand down her face, and I could see she was trying to keep her tears inside, too.

"Distance. Like twenty-four hundred miles." I sat back in my chair, feeling drained. Giving up.

"Yeah. Like that." Her gaze dropped, as if she couldn't look at me.

All I could do was nod. I picked up my fork and took a bite of my eggs, not tasting them and not wanting them, but knowing I had to eat. She did the same. After a few moments, we tried to turn the conversation to other things, and she still somehow made me laugh with stories from her tour. I already missed this so much.

Outside of the restaurant, we hugged for what seemed like five entire minutes. I wanted to feel every piece of her, feel her heart beat against mine. When we finally pulled away, I kept my hands at her waist. She put her palm gently against my cheek and I leaned into it, closing my eyes and missing her already.

"Break a leg tomorrow night. You're going to knock their socks off."

I nodded, trying to smile. "Thank you. And I'll see you after?"

"I wouldn't miss it."

We kissed each other on the cheek and I was stilled by the pain of it all. Before she walked away, she squeezed my hand. Then she turned and disappeared around the corner.

It wasn't our final goodbye, but it sure felt like it.

TWENTY

Honestly, I kind of blacked out.

I knew that the show had happened, but I didn't remember doing it. Like when you're driving home and your mind goes blank and you somehow find yourself in the driveway anyway.

I exited stage left after the last number and noted the faces of the stagehands and dressers I passed, beaming at me. I felt my castmates file offstage behind me and we all began hugging as the music swelled and turned into our curtain call cue. The audience was cheering loudly over the bow music.

My heart began to pound as I came back to myself, as the ensemble members went out for their bows. Had I done it? Had I done my job? Had I brought Cassandra to life?

Jeffrey squeezed my shoulder on his way past me to the stage for his bow. Upstage, he spread his arms wide, as campy as his character, and walked downstage to wild applause.

Steph and Dev went next, coming from stage right. I watched them take their bows together and took a deep, cleansing breath. Certainly the audience would stop cheering and start booing when I stepped out, right?

The company separated and threw their arms to center. That was my cue.

I plastered on a smile, ignored the queasiness in my stomach, and walked out to the swell of the reprise of "I Am Standing". I strode purposefully to center and turned.

Like a punch to the chest, the cheering hit me and the audience leapt to their feet. Dazed, I walked downstage and took a bow to deafening shouts and applause. I straightened and I felt tears spring into my eyes.

This was every moment I had ever dreamed.

Stepping back, I joined the line with Dev and Steph. The cast followed me as I acknowledged the orchestra and the tech booth. Then we all took one another's hands and bowed as one, once, twice, three times, until the curtain finally closed.

Once the audience was out of view, it felt as though a bubble of silence had settled over all of us. We all looked around at one another and then exploded into hugs and whooping and congratulations as we tumbled together down the stairs to our dressing rooms.

§

"You ready?" Toby said.

I straightened my gold, strapless cocktail dress and nodded, feeling more nervous for this party than for the opening itself. I glanced at Andrea.

She took me by the shoulders gently and said without hesitation, "You are a superstar." I cracked a nervous smile and felt much better.

"Let's go." Toby held his arm out to me and I looped my own through it. He led me to the balcony above the lobby in the theater and I was once again struck by the opulence of the space. Before we were noticed, I took in the sight of the guests in fancy dresses and suits, some even wearing tuxedos. Champagne was being passed by servers carrying fancy golden trays and others weaved in and out with tiny, fussy hors d'oeuvres.

Folks seemed happy, relaxed, and most were talking animatedly. I couldn't see one sour face in the sea. Some of my castmates were being fawned over, and I spotted my family near the bar. I smirked. Of course they'd found that first. Then I noticed Kat, who at the same time looked up. I gave her a tiny wave. Grinning widely, she sent up a "whoop!" and began clapping, nearly spilling her champagne.

All eyes were on us now, and the applause was once again deafening. Toby squeezed my arm and the three of us turned and made our way down the grand staircase. Soaring on the high that I was, Alex hadn't yet crossed my mind. Then we stepped onto the floor and it hit me like a brick landing in my stomach. The only face I wanted to see was hers.

But I couldn't think about that. I was immediately swept away into a fray of glittering people who wanted selfies, donors who wanted my ear, and any number of people who just wanted to congratulate us. Someone shoved a champagne flute in my hand and when it was empty, it got immediately replaced. Somewhere in the whirlwind, I saw Kat and Dev, and met Jeffrey's partner. Steph dragged me over to meet her college friends. Nathan, my agent, had flown in and when he caught me up in a tight hug, he whispered, "Told you so." Dr. James was there with his wife, and they were both full of praise. I gave him a big squeeze, thanking him for his help.

A whirl of compliments swished around me, and I was humbled and elated for the accolades. I knew it would feel good to have my work acknowledged after so many years, but I didn't know it would be so intoxicating. I accepted the praise and thanked everyone sincerely as Toby and Andrea pulled me in all different directions. I hadn't even been able to say hello to my family.

It felt like I was living someone else's life, a fairy tale, and I was Cinderella.

And then I saw her, standing at a cocktail table across the room, all on her own. She looked ravishing. Absolutely devastating. My Alex. Her hair was smoothed down sleek and crowned with a thin sparkly headband, making her look like a flapper girl. She wore a black leather jumpsuit, which hugged her curves in all the right places, and when she turned I almost gasped. It was completely backless.

A quick flashback ran through my mind. My lips on her shoulder blade, my arms curled around her from behind, her gasp as I cupped her breast with one hand and my other hand traveled lower.

I shook myself out of that particular reverie and she turned her head. Our gazes met. Across a glittering party. Practically forbidden love.

Maybe I was in a fairy tale.

Together, we stepped forward and as we made our way across the room, I was intercepted by a familiar voice.

"Little One!" My dad scooped me up into the tightest hug he'd ever given me.

I laughed against his shoulder. "Hi, Dad." When I pulled away and looked into his eyes, they were filled with tears.

"Oh honey, we're just so proud." He sniffed and pulled an ancient handkerchief from his obviously new suit.

"Hey, this is new. You look so handsome, Daddio." I fussed with his lapel.

He dabbed at his eyes while I was embraced by Tom and Josh, then Angie and Savannah. Sam was last.

"Pretty great work up there, little sister." He picked me up in a crushing hug and over his shoulder, I saw Alex walking away. My smile faded. Sam put me down and grinned full force down into my face. It flickered when he took note of my expression. The rest of my family were distracted by introductions to Toby and Andrea, and Sam asked me in a low voice, "Is she here?"

I nodded and bit my lip. "I can't get close to her. I keep getting intercepted. I barely got to you."

Sam squeezed my shoulder and began to say something else, but then Andrea began to introduce herself. And then I was pulled into a discussion of my character with my dad and Tom and then I was pulled over to Steph's parents who had *just been dying to meet you* and then it was Dev and Jeffrey posing in front of the step-and-repeat and then it was more accolades from more strangers until finally, another hour later, I excused myself to go to the restroom. I scanned the room for Alex, who must have been watching me, because I managed to meet her eyes and hopefully communicated that I wanted her to follow me.

As I was drying my hands, the door opened and she walked in. Immediately, I crumbled. I forgot everything but her. We caught eyes in the mirror and the world around us seemed to stop. The glittering party vanished, the champagne dried up, it was just the two of us in this opulent powder room, in what we both knew was the last time we would talk. I turned to her.

"Paige, I'm in awe."

"Thank you."

"You were magnificent. You were glowing. I couldn't keep my eyes off you. You're a star."

I stared down at my gold heels. "Thank you," I whispered again. Then I gave a scoffing laugh. "I have never said thank you so many times before in my life."

She chuckled. "I bet. Well, you deserve every word. Truly spectacular."

I met her sweet gaze again and was not surprised to see her eyes swimming with tears. I stepped toward her and pulled her into an embrace. She twirled some of my hair into her hand and I let my hands caress the soft skin of her back. I couldn't resist kissing her bare shoulder, and I heard her take a deep gasping breath. So entwined, I said, "I love you, Alex."

Her hand tightened in my hair, her other flat against the small of my back pressed harder. "I love you, too."

I was trying to contain myself, if only to preserve my makeup, when the door flew open. Andrea took in the scene and an understanding expression crossed her face. Alex and I broke apart and I looked to the ceiling to keep my tears at bay.

"I'm sorry, Paige, there are a couple of investors I need you to meet." Her voice was quiet, full of sympathy.

I nodded and turned to the mirror. I still looked fine, except for the misery in my expression. Alex stood behind me and our eyes met in the glass. I turned, and as I walked toward the door, I grasped her hand and squeezed. "Don't leave without saying goodbye."

She nodded, clearly trying to hold back tears. I swallowed the lump in my throat and left.

But it wasn't to be. My presence was demanded all night by one person or another. Any other time I would have been more than happy to talk up the show and my cast, and Andrea and Toby, too. I hoped I didn't sound fake. I meant every word I was saying, but my heart was shattering at the same time. Two completely dichotomous emotions were flowing through me: elation and devastation.

I tried to make my way to her a dozen times, but each time I was pulled away. The look on her face said she understood, but I couldn't stand the pain behind her eyes. I wanted to say goodbye to her properly. I wanted to tell her she was the love of my life.

But time was passing too quickly, and I could see that she was going to rip the Band-Aid off when I was pulled away just a few feet from her, yet again. Over the head of an ancient little man who was apparently going to invest in the Broadway run, I watched Alex walk sadly toward the door. I smiled and nodded as the man went on and on.

When she reached the exit, Alex raised her hand up at me, her expression soft and sad and furious all at once. I'm sure my face betrayed my pain to everyone who could see it, but the old man kept chattering, oblivious. I raised my hand and waved once. A half smile appeared on her face and she turned.

Then she was gone.

TWENTY-ONE

The glittering reception lasted another half an hour after Alex disappeared. I begged off from celebrating with the cast at a bar, who were going to wait for the reviews to come in. I had already done too much talking, and after what I'd just gone through, I wasn't going to tempt fate. And we had to do this the next night. And the next. From now on, Mondays were my only days off.

When I arrived home, I stripped off the party dress and put on the Cubs *v.* Brewers tee. On my bed in my underwear, I opened my laptop. I wanted to write about my first opening night, because I knew that my brain would try to only remember the sad parts with Alex. As I sat and typed about the feelings it gave me and the people I'd met and how happy I was, the realization of what had just occurred really hit me: I had done it. I had achieved my actual dream. While distracted by Alex and making myself numb enough that I wouldn't puke from nerves before the show, I hadn't let it sink in that every dream I'd ever had finally came true that night.

Different tears came to me now. Jesus, I felt like I'd been crying for weeks. But these were tears of gratitude and joy. I let it all go, alone in this stupid little studio. I flung myself on my mattress and gave way to the dramatics. I felt so good. Honored. Loved. Taken care of. The adoration I felt for the entire company of *On Her Own* burst inside of my chest like starlight and coursed through my veins. It's as if I hadn't allowed myself to truly feel this until the show opened.

Gulping, I sat up and wiped my eyes on my shirt, then hunted around for my box of tissues. Blotting the tears from my face, I groped for my phone and texted Toby.

> Just had a full- body-breakdowny-all-consuming wonderful cry. Thank you for allowing me to feel this. Thank you for believing in me. Thank you for this life. Thank you thank you thank you.

I don't think I had ever been that effusive with him, so I hoped he wouldn't be weirded out by my middle-of-the-night- seemingly-drunk dramatics. He responded immediately with a heart emoji. And a link to the review from the *Chicago Tribune*.

He would never send me the link if it were bad. I leapt up from the bed staring at my phone screen, the only light I had on. I paced. Hesitated. Groaned. Threw the phone on the loveseat.

It had to be good.

It had to be.

He wouldn't send it if it wasn't.

I picked up my phone again, clicked the link, and immediately closed my eyes. Then I opened one of them, squinting, hoping that if I only peeked at it, the review would be good.

> For a brand-new musical, there was blessedly little to nitpick. *On Her Own* is a spectacle of lights and sets and costumes, but do not discount the story. It is a tale as old as time, and yet somehow, Toby Anderson has breathed new life into the story of a woman finding herself.
>
> It is moving in ways this reviewer did not expect. The score sweeps you through Cassandra's journey, the funny moments are hilarious, the touching moments will bring a tear to your eye, and in the deft and talented hands of Paige Parker, Cassandra comes to life. Parker is effortless and eminently watchable, with a face like a forties movie star and a voice that will bring you to your knees. Watch out Broadway: You have a genuine star on your hands.

The review was glowing. Utterly, completely glowing. The only issue the reviewer had was some technical stuff. But the story, he loved. I gasped for breath and of course I began to cry again. Apparently, I was going to cry forever. I sent Toby a heart emoji back and read the review again.

And again.

And maybe again. One more time.

For luck.

In the morning--well, the early afternoon--I was greeted with dozens of texts and a missed call from my dad. I hurried to call him back. We'd barely gotten a chance to say goodbye the night before.

"That's my superstar!"

I laughed aloud. "Morning, Dad."

"We're all in the car driving back home now. Wanted to give you a call to say how proud we are. Again."

I was on the car's Bluetooth, so they must have been in one of my brothers' SUVs. Dad's ancient Honda could never. Everyone shouted their congratulations again and I basked in their love and accolades.

"Thank you all so much for being there. I'm sorry we didn't get to talk much. I would have had breakfast with you this morning, but--"

Tom spoke up. "You need your beauty sleep if you're going to sing like that every night! Holy shit, kid, you're incredible. I knew you could sing, but I didn't know you could do *that*."

"We're going to bring the kids down for a show, okay?" Savannah said.

"I'd love that. Just tell me when and I'll make sure you're taken care of."

"Look at you, our famous sister," said Josh, his voice full of pride.

"Quit. I'm not famous." I rolled my eyes and sat up in bed, stretching.

"You're gonna be!" Angie called from what sounded like the backseat.

I smiled to myself and let them chatter for a while, loving them deeply. I would miss them bunches when I moved back to New York.

My voice needed resting when we hung up. I ran an almost unbearably hot shower and let the steam fill my lungs. It was only then that I let Alex enter my thoughts. I groaned aloud as I felt myself want to cry again. It was almost laughable at this point. And I wanted to keep my voice healthy, so I only allowed the sadness in temporarily. I couldn't stop seeing her face, those big brown eyes reflecting the misery I felt. And then the turn of her back as she walked out the door.

I had to let her go now. I didn't want to let her go. But I didn't have a choice. She was leaving. I was leaving. It wasn't meant to be.

I put on sweatpants and a hoodie, blow-dried my hair, and began making myself some pasta. Memories of Alex stirring her grandmother's sauce ran through my mind as I added oregano and basil to my sad attempt to replicate it. Her lips around the wooden spoon, then on my own--

A knock at my door made me jump.

Alex?

I flung it open without even looking through the peephole, forgetting everything I'd ever learned about living alone in a city.

Dev and Kat stood smiling at the door, a take-out bag in Dev's hands.

"Hello, superstar."

I smiled, though mildly disappointed. "Hey, buddies. Did you make out again last night?"

In unison, they both deadpanned, "Never again."

I chuckled and moved aside so they could come in.

Kat observed the tiny kitchen and the tiny stove and the sad attempt at sauce. She cocked an eyebrow at me. "She's trying to cook, Dev."

He set the bag on the coffee table and moved over to the stove where he picked up the spoon and tasted the sauce. Licking his lips, he turned to me. "Honey. No."

We all burst into laughter and Dev scraped the sauce into the garbage where it belonged, turned off the burner, and tossed the saucepan in the sink. As we settled around the coffee table, opening containers of salad and grilled salmon, Dev said, "What on earth were you trying to make pasta sauce for? You're a terrible cook. They have that stuff in jars, you know."

"Alex," Kat said without hesitating. I glanced up at her sheepishly. She smiled and tossed a cherry tomato in her mouth. "Just because we don't live together anymore doesn't mean that I don't know you like the back of my hand."

I gave her a half smile and reached for my takeout container. "Thank you for saving me from eating that." I looked over at the clock. We had two hours until Dev and I had to be at the theater for mic checks. "Are you coming again tonight?"

"No, I foolishly booked a ten o'clock flight out of here. I have to get back. Rehearsal on Monday and I want to rest tomorrow."

"Ah."

A strange, pulsing silence fell and I didn't know how to fill it. My sadness seemed to permeate the apartment, coupled with my joy at the way the show was received. I was going back and forth between these emotions like a ping pong ball.

Dev looked into my face searchingly and then finally said, "How was seeing Alex last night?"

Sighing, I put down my fork and buried my face in my hands. "Wonderful. Devastating. It's off completely. She's going to L.A. I'm going back to New York. We love each other. I will likely always love her. And there's nothing I can do about it."

Dev and Kat exchanged a look.

"What?"

"Long distance is hard. But it's not worth trying?" Kat said.

"What would be the point? Our careers are clear across the country from one another. If there was an end date to that, then yes, I would try it. But there isn't. Long distance doesn't work forever. And it *would* be forever."

Another silence. Then another thought came to me. "But maybe I won't get asked to do the Broadway run." I both thrilled at this and despised the thought of someone else stepping into Cassandra on Broadway. My god, I could not get a handle on my emotions.

Dev rolled his eyes magnificently. "That is not going to happen. You are the heart and soul of this show. There's no way they won't ask you to stay."

"Well. Thank you. But if they didn't, I could go to L.A."

"And do *theater*?" Dev, a purist, I knew, was appalled by the thought.

"Or try my hand at on-camera stuff." I shrugged.

Kat looked at me like I was spewing nonsense. Which I was. "You're not going to L.A."

"How are you so confident?"

"Because I saw the show, Paige. You are spectacular. And so are you," she tossed a wry smile at Dev, who had opened his mouth to demand a compliment, too. He glowed at her words. "Both of you are taking this show to New York, mark my words."

"But if I don't," I persisted.

She rolled her eyes. "Fine. If you don't, we can discuss you moving to L.A."

"I need your permission?"

Kat looked to Dev, eyes wide. They looked at me, and again in unison, cried, "Yes!"

We fell into giggles and finished our meals, though the daydream of moving to the West Coast to be with Alex sustained me. I was in a lighter mood as I did my mic check and then put on my costume and makeup. I saw us walking up the boardwalk in Venice Beach and hiking in the mountains. We could get a dog. We could wake up next to each other every morning. I bet my agent would love having me out there. I could find work.

I went to sleep after another good show that night, California dreaming.

§

After a very successful opening weekend and several more glowing reviews, I met Toby and Andrea for coffee on Monday afternoon. We ordered and took our lattes to a table, where they sat facing me, grins spreading wide across both of their faces. I had thought they'd just wanted to debrief about the show but was starting to guess that wasn't the case at all.

"Paige," Andrea started, unable to contain herself. "We've talked to our necessary people. And your necessary people. But we wanted to be the ones to tell you."

A fluttering began in my stomach and moved up to my chest.

"You have to keep this to yourself for now. Tell absolutely no one. We will be making formal announcements when the time is right," Toby added.

"And we mean no one. Not your dad, not your best friend, not Al-- No one," Andrea finished.

I barely even registered that she had almost mentioned Alex. I nodded, my stomach now apparently training for the Olympics. "Okay."

Andrea and Toby smiled at each other, then beamed right at me. Toby reached over and grasped my hand.

"We're taking you to Broadway."

Everything disappeared. I braced my hands on the table in front of me and took deep breaths. The coffee shop swirled around me, the noises muted, the lights fuzzy. I closed my eyes, took one last breath, and waited for the world to right itself. Opening my eyes, the shop came rushing back, including the two people practically combusting with joy across from me.

A smile burst across my face. A chortle burbled out of me, low at first and then full and real and loud. We were getting stares. They began laughing, too. And somehow, though I noticed Toby's eyes fill and Andrea sniffling a bit, for the first time in weeks, I didn't cry. I couldn't believe this was happening to me. As it had after opening night, reality hit me.

I was going to star on Broadway.

"We're sending a contract over to your agent this week. You're ours, sweetheart."

"And I didn't have to fight anyone this time," Toby said sweetly. "Now everyone can see what I saw."

Overcome, I tried to tell them what this meant to me. "Thank you. Thank you both. Obviously, I couldn't have done it without you, I wouldn't be the performer I am without either of you. Andrea, you're the best director I have ever worked with. And Toby..." I met his eyes. He squeezed my hand and I knew words were no longer necessary. This was a friendship that would last a lifetime.

I asked some questions about the timeline. Our final performance here in Chicago would be on New Year's Eve, then we would have a brief break to get settled back in New York. They would take care of whatever casting issues would arise, deal with any music and book issues, come up with another rehearsal schedule, and the hope, tentatively, was for an opening at the Nederlander Theater on 41st Street a year from now. The theater could change, the cast could change, the schedule could change, but my role would not. I was in as Cassandra, whatever happened. That was non-negotiable, according to Toby.

I nearly skipped home.

Later, I let it hit me that New York was solidly in my future. And L.A. was not. I was getting good at this compartmentalizing thing. This was it, the time to let Alex go. I wanted to tell her so she could also let go of the hope, but I didn't want to break our radio silence pact. And Toby and Andrea had made me swear up and down a thousand times that I wouldn't say anything. So I didn't, as badly as I wanted to.

I was getting everything I had worked for, everything I had ever wanted.

Everything but her.

Twenty-Two

As the run of the show continued, I managed to keep my big secret. We dealt with the glitches: a forgotten prop here, a dropped line there, a voice cracking every once in a while. And I took care of my voice as we settled into the rhythm of performing every night. My family came again around Thanksgiving, with the kids this time. I was bursting with my news, but I kept my promise as we moved into the winter. And Chicago winter wind was no joke. December turned cold and I wore two layers of pants on my way to the theater every day. I couldn't risk my muscles seizing up onstage, even though I stretched and warmed up.

I didn't hear a word from Alex, our moratorium on talking absolute, apparently. The pain seemed to lessen until I let myself think about it. Then it was impossible not to miss her.

On Wednesday, the week before Christmas, between the matinee and evening shows, a company meeting was called. We all wandered to the stage, chatting, sharing granola, and sipping from water bottles. Company meetings weren't rare. I had an inkling as to what it was, but the rest of the cast probably thought there was a safety issue or something. Something about the fly lines or a prop knife. We draped ourselves around the stage, stretching and leaning against one another.

Andrea clapped her hands and we gave her our attention. "Thank you everyone, settle down. Thank you for giving us your time." A quiver of confusion ran through us. She was being much more formal than usual, almost stoic.

"As you all know, we wanted to take this show to Broadway from the beginning. And we now have to tell you..."

She paused and we all leaned forward. I swallowed hard, puzzled by her tone. What was she about to say? We weren't getting the run after all? An investor pulled out? I could see us all starting to freak out a little, worried glances being exchanged. Was I going to lose my first starring role?

"We will open next October at the Nederlander! And it is our hope that schedules align and we'll be able to take all of you with us."

The collective sigh of relief was extreme, followed by elated cheers.

I caught Andrea's eye and she winked at me. Grinning from ear to ear, I shook my head and wagged my finger at her. Sneaky girl.

My castmates, meanwhile, were losing their minds. Now that the run was solidified, the joy we felt at not having to say goodbye to our beautiful show was intense. We hugged and chattered and Andrea said a few more words, but it was all a blur. Then we had the evening show to prepare for so we trooped downstairs to our dressing rooms.

Dev appeared in my doorway. He pointed a finger at me like a prosecuting attorney. "You knew," he accused.

I guess I had been a little more subdued than I would have been had I not known. I threw my hands up innocently and smirked.

He gasped. "And you didn't tell me."

I placed a hand over my heart. "I was sworn to secrecy."

He rolled his eyes and tossed himself down into the big armchair. We met gazes in my mirror. "I told you so." He was gloating.

"Hush." I grinned widely and touched up my eyeliner.

"Never."

"Back to New York." I was looking forward to getting home and had tried to make my peace with Alex not being a part of my future. I didn't like it. It hurt to think about all that we'd never have. But I was trying to move forward.

"We're going to have the best time." Dev stood and walked over to me. He put his arms around my shoulders and rested his head next to mine. We looked at each other in the mirror. "I'm so glad we have each other. And Paige. There will be another Alex." He kissed the top of my head and left the room, closing the door.

I put my blush brush down and watched as my eyes filled with sadness. There would never be another Alex. Dates, yes. Passionate affairs, yes. Loves, yes. But never--*never*--another Alex.

Happily, Christmas was on a Monday that year and I was able to spend it with my family. After the Sunday matinee on Christmas Eve, I took the train up to Wisconsin and spent a lovely time in the warmth of my dad's house, sitting by the fire, baking cookies with the kids, and teasing my brothers. It was a necessary break before the last week of shows.

On the train back down to Chicago on Tuesday morning, my phone vibrated. I had been gazing out of the window, listening to music, mentally preparing for stepping back onstage that night.

> Just saw the news. So well deserved. I'm really proud of you. Congratulations.

My heart skipped one beat, and then several. Alex. The news must have been broken on *Playbill*. But Broadway news wasn't widely known, so she must have been looking for it. Googling me. A sensation like grief sliced through me at this thought. I loved that she was thinking about me. I hated that there was nothing I could do about it.

My phone vibrated again.

> Is it silly and selfish to say I kind of hoped you'd move to LA to take a stab at film?

I covered my mouth with my hand, wanting to both laugh and weep. Another text.

> To be clear, I'm really glad you're not. And that this is happening for you. I'm sad for ME, is what I'm saying.

I laughed out loud and got a look from the older man sitting across the aisle.

> Fuck, now I'm texting you four times in a row and you probably hate me for breaking our pact of silence. Well, deal with it. I'm happy for you.

God, this girl. My heart. My whole entire heart. I typed back.

> I'm really glad to hear from you. And it's not silly and selfish at all. It crossed my mind.

I hesitated, then texted again.

> Have you moved yet?

The little bubbles jumped up and down, telling me she was typing. They stopped. Then they started again. What was she trying to say? I wasn't sure how I would feel if she had moved without trying to say goodbye. Finally:

> Not yet. Contract stuff still being worked out. I don't want to bite the bullet until I have to.

She was still in Chicago. Still just a few minutes away from me. I couldn't handle that. I wanted to see her so badly but hesitated to ask her to coffee. Then I thought *fuck it* and typed again.

> Do you want to say goodbye before I go back to New York? I leave on the second.

Immediately, she responded.

> Of course.

I sent a heart emoji, but she didn't respond after that. Maybe that was too much. But I didn't dwell on it. I wanted her to have my heart, but it wasn't meant to be. So she could have this tiny cartoon version instead.

What a sad substitution.

Maybe when I was back in New York, back to my regular life, I wouldn't feel so sad all the time. Maybe I could really move on once I was out of the city with all of the memories of us.

§

Absolute chaos. That is the only way to describe the raucous New Year's Eve show. It was closing night and we were headed to Broadway. The audience's energy was electric. They hollered and clapped more than any audience had before, and after intermission, forget it. Everyone seemed to have downed a couple of glasses of wine in quick succession.

It was wonderful.

When I took my final bow and led the cast in the rest, the standing ovation lasted a full five minutes. I was beaming at the end of it. And I was ready. Just ready. I was ready to ring in the new year with my company, ready to move back to my home and Kat, and ready to put this amazing, devastating, wonderful year behind me. I was so grateful for everything I'd gone through this year, no matter how gut-wrenching. I found the truth, found love, found new bonds with my family, and found myself. Perhaps someday, I'd get my happy ending, too. But for now, I was thrilled to get Cassandra's.

It was time.

The atmosphere backstage after the show was festive. Before changing, Dev poured shots of whiskey and we all toasted each other. We left our dressing room doors open and talk-yelled about the pride we had in our show, about the party we were going to, and what everyone was wearing. I stepped into a long sleeved, backless, silver sequined jumpsuit. I needed to give my body a break, so I slipped on a pair of flats. I left on most of my show makeup and kept my hair cascading down my back in Cassandra's waves. I looked in the mirror and blew her a kiss.

"See you soon, sister," I told her. She helped me in ways I couldn't even fathom yet. I bundled my winter coat around myself and belted it. Taking a deep breath, I met Dev and Steph and we walked out of the stage door to more intense cheering.

Since the show had announced it was going to Broadway, the stage door crowds had been intense. The Cadillac Palace's stage door came out at the loading dock, so instead of an alley, there was a space where two large trucks could park in front of the garage doors. Tonight, it was filled to the brim with screaming audience members behind metal barricades. When we stepped out, flashes started going off and my name was yelled. I walked down the line, smiling, taking selfies, and signing *Playbills*. The joy that washed over me as I did this was too much to describe. The eyes of the young girls and women in front of me filled my heart, knowing that they saw Cassandra as their hero and that I had the privilege of bringing her to life.

Snow had begun to fall in large, heavy flakes, and I was ready for a glass of champagne. Ten minutes, then fifteen, passed. I was still taking selfies and signing autographs, but I was nearing the end of the line. I glanced around, hoping at least one of my castmates would wait for me so we could go to the party together.

And then there she was.

Under the El, leaning against an old-fashioned lamppost, a little farther up the street.

Alex.

My whole body reacted. Suddenly, I couldn't hear anything but the beat of my own heart. Then my hands began to sweat. I stood, frozen with a Sharpie over a *Playbill*, my mouth in an 'O'. She was here. Right in front of me.

All the noise came rushing back and I finished signing my name. I moved very quickly through the last few people and said goodbye. I turned toward Alex, who raised her hand in greeting, her sweet face full of joy. Slowly, as though moving through sand, I made my way to her. Hope bloomed in my chest because I couldn't imagine her being here for any reason other than we were going to be able to make this work.

I stopped just short of touching her and she hit me full force with that incredible smile.

I shook my head, grinning back, my heart hammering. "I thought we were meeting up tomorrow afternoon."

She shrugged, mischievous. "This couldn't wait." She bit her bottom lip and it took everything in my power not to pull her into my arms.

"What is it? What are you doing here?" I demanded.

She took a step closer. "The L.A. contract. It fell through."

My breath quickened and I felt the world stop around us. Perfect snowflakes were landing on her shoulders and her winter hat. The train rumbled past above us, the noise deafening.

She took another step and put her hand on mine. She ran her thumb over my lifeline. I looked at her with wide eyes.

"There was another show that wanted me. But it was just a pilot, they weren't picked up for a season yet. My agent and I decided not to take the chance on the pilot-only offer. There was no guarantee that it would get to series. So we took the L.A. job instead, but it didn't work out." She paused, her smile radiant. "Then the pilot got picked up for a season."

I squeezed her fingers, feeling a rush of excitement. "What does this mean?"

"It films in New York." Her voice caught and my breath hitched at the same time. Her warm brown eyes met mine, vulnerable and hopeful and full of love.

"It's a done deal," she almost whispered. "Signed on the dotted line."

Urgently, I pulled her to me, my hand cradling her cheek, the other gripping her waist. She draped her arms around my neck and I brushed her nose with mine. "You're moving to New York?"

She nodded, a smile spreading across her perfect face as I melted my lips onto hers. The train above us rumbled by as we fell into each other again. Snow swirled, the scream of the train sounded like music, and suddenly we were laughing and kissing at the same time. Her hands tangled in my hair and I grasped her waist like she was a life preserver and I was drowning.

I pulled back and we touched foreheads, both of us beaming. I couldn't seem to stop my joyous laughter. But when I gazed into her eyes, I was met with deep concern. She averted her gaze down to our hands, clasped together.

"Can you forgive me? For leaving you? For not taking the New York job in the first place and taking a chance on us? I wasn't strong enough. One of my favorite things about you is how brave you are. And I wasn't. I should have been. I'm so sorry. Paige, I love you more than anyone I've ever known. Please forgive me."

I pulled back a little and tilted her chin so our eyes met.

"There's nothing to forgive," I said in all honesty. Because there wasn't. She was here, now, and that is what mattered. I brushed my lips on hers, no longer laughing. "I love you, Alex. And I'm going to love you forever."

In response, she took my face in her hands and kissed me deeply, tenderly. The golden thread between us strengthened and knotted, shining brightly. Permanently. And then, as it had with our first kiss, but with more clarity now, our life together rushed through my mind. I saw tour buses and backstage green rooms, lounging together before performances. The day we'd move in together, meshing our lives into one. Our small apartment where Sammy would grow old and cranky and the little dog curled up on the sofa. The warm and inviting home where we would come together as often as we could. Alex sitting at front row cabaret tables when I performed solo shows. The Tonys red carpet where we sparkled in glittery outfits, holding hands. New York in the fall, Cubs games in the summer, visits to Wisconsin and the suburbs.

Our first real fight, our raised voices and real tears. Then our first real forgiveness, when neither of us would run. When we both decided to stay, over and over again. The inside jokes that made us laugh so hard we couldn't breathe. Standing on the shore of Lake Michigan, Alex down on one knee, her eyes sparkling with hope. The walk down the aisle, the candlelight and romance, the scent of lilacs, and our first kiss as wives. The sunset in Bali, drippy with gold, the softness of her skin. The wanting and hoping, the paperwork, and finally the announcement and the beautiful baby's arrival.

Faster still, the images came. Photoshoots. Diners on the road. Curtain calls. Writer's rooms. New houses. Cribs and baby toys. Rehearsals. Kindergarten. Comedy specials. Emergency rooms. Ballet recitals. Graduations. Reunions. Rowdy red carpets, flashes everywhere, and quiet moments in sunlight. Everything wrapped in our forever love.

I saw it all in that kiss. This wasn't my happy ending. It was our happy beginning. And when I pulled back and we gazed into each other's eyes, I knew she saw it, too. She brushed my nose with hers. I took her hand and we turned toward our next adventure together, for the first of a million times.

fin

About the Author

With over ten years of wedding planning experience and a lifetime onstage, Avery Easton knows romance. When she was seven years old, in a pink Snoopy notebook, she began writing stories and hasn't stopped since. If she's not reading or writing, you can find her cross stitching or belting out showtunes. She lives in Chicago with her husband and two adorable cats. Follow her on Instagram @averyeastonwrites.

* * * *

If I Told You is available as an eBook from Uncial Press. Uncial Press brings you extraordinary fiction, non-fiction and poetry. Put a world of reading in your pocket.
www.uncialpress.com

Made in the USA
Monee, IL
13 June 2021